THE ILLUSIONEER

and Other Tales

THE ILLUSIONEER

and Other Tales

THE ADVENTURES OF VIOLA STEWART
JOURNAL #3

KAREN J CARLISLE

The Illusioneer and Other Tales
The Adventures of Viola Stewart Journal #3
Copyright © 2017 Karen J Carlisle
Second Edition © 2022 Karen J Carlisle

Cover design, photography artwork ©2022 by Karen J Carlisle
Icons and internal artwork: © 2015 by Karen J Carlisle
ISBN: 978-0-9944850-8-3

A catalogue record for this book is available from the National Library of Australia

Also available separately as eBook.

This book is written in British English.
Printed in Australia.
First Edition, 2017
First Revision 2018
Second Edition 2022

Typeset in Times Roman 10pt.

Published by Kraken Publishing.
www.krakenpublishing.com

For Susan, who pushed me.
For David and Morgan, who encouraged me.
For Viola, who bore my pain.

Contents

Bonus Excerpt

From the Depths

Chapter 1:
A Holiday at the Beach

The lace curtain fluttered in the sea breeze. Dappled sunlight danced across the table and skittered over the page of Viola's book. She glanced out of the window. A family group strolled along the sand. A small boy chased the receding water. Only one bathing machine had ventured into the sea, its occupant hidden from view.

Few holiday-makers braved the North Sea so late in the season. And those who did so most likely desired the health benefits of the icy waters.

Light flickered across the enamelled surface of her untouched tea tray. Gold glinted along the oval rim, highlighting a set of hieroglyphs partly obscured by the teapot and saucer. A stylised eye stared back.

The hair stood up on the back of Viola's neck. A vision of a vacant-eyed falcon flickered across her mind. She squeezed her eye shut, trying to suppress the memory of her last adventure. A woman's voice whispered her name.

Viola shook her head. The hallucinations were less frequent, now the vestiges of toxins were fading, but still just as unnerving.

She draped a shawl over the tray and opened her eye.

Perhaps if she ignored it...? She swung her legs over the arm of the camel-back sofa, letting her stockinged feet dangle over the edge, and continued reading Arthur's book: Ram Singh had arrived at Cloomber Hall and things were afoot.

The curtain whipped at her shoulder and slapped on the stack of books on the side table, dislodging the pile of letters beside them. One fluttered to the ground.

Viola frowned. She snapped the book shut and reached down to retrieve the papers, and placed them on her lap. The edges were dog-eared, the wax seal on the envelope cracked; most had crumbled away, leaving red stains on the envelope paper. She re-folded the letter and slipped it into the square envelope. She had read it a hundred times. It was all that remained of her sister, Anne. Her last words burned in her heart:

'I now take my leave of Edinburgh and my family's favour to make my own way in the world and to avoid any scandal.'

Viola twisted the engagement ring on her finger. It felt strangely cold. Her heart thickened in her chest, pushing on her throat. How could she contemplate her future, not knowing her sister's fate?

She grabbed the heavy linen curtain, unhooked it from the metal tie back and yanked it across the window. She snatched up her book. It was easier to forget one's troubles when lost in a fictional world of mystery and magic.

A faint tap on the door behind Viola caught her attention. She turned a page and ignored the interruption.

"Miss?" Polly knocked again.

Viola took a deep breath, adjusted her eyepatch and lowered her feet onto the floor. Polly wouldn't leave until she was ensured Viola was adhering to Doctor's orders.

"Come in, Polly."

Polly surveyed the darkened room and raised an eyebrow. "You should know better than to read in the dark, Miss." She adjusted the bundle of clothing draped over one arm, pulled open the linen curtain and slid down the window sash.

Viola turned a page and mumbled in reply.

Polly straightened the pile of books, paying particular attention to the well-worn bundle of letters. "And how is Mr Fothergill-West faring with the General's daughter?"

"Hmmm..." Viola turned another page, hoping Polly would soon abandon her latest attempt to drag her from her solitude.

Polly glanced at the letter lying on Viola's lap and cleared her throat.

"Should I organise a table for dinner, Miss? I hear there's smoked salmon and Nesselrode Pudding. Doctor Collins loves Nesselrode pudding."

"I'll be dining in my rooms tonight, Polly," replied Viola.

Polly hovered beside Viola's chair. "May I speak plainly, Miss?"

"Of course."

"Miss Viola..." A wrinkle flashed across Polly's forehead. "It isn't healthy to sit in the dark, all alone. Perhaps a quick dip in the sea will rouse you out of this melancholia? Doctor Collins has recommended cold water bathing as part of your convalescence regime." Polly unfurled the garments from her arm and held them up for Viola to examine. A navy-blue skirt and bodice, with matching pantaloons. Thick woollen stockings remained draped on Polly's arm.

Viola straightened up in her chair.

"It's a bit short, isn't it?" she asked.

"It's the fashion in bathing attire this year. I'm sure Doctor Collins would find it agreeable."

A faint smile flickered over Viola's lips. "I'm sure he would."

"Then, it's settled. I'll order you a carriage. I'll have your nerve tonic ready for when you return."

"Perhaps I'll meet this monster the locals whisper about?" Viola closed her book.

"The Lurker?" Polly's arms dropped by her side. A stocking fluttered to the floor. "Oh dear, I'd forgotten about that."

"Don't fret, Polly. There's no such thing as monsters." Viola laughed. "Perhaps you should try some of Doctor Collins' tonic to calm your nerves?"

"What about the Loch Ness Monster?" asked Polly.

"Oh, the Scots love a good tale. The local publican probably dresses up in a diving suit to scare the tourists. Then they all have a laugh in the alehouse." Viola gathered up the bathing suit and held it up to her shoulders. "I do like a good mystery." She examined her silk-stockinged toes. Wool would be so cumbersome in the water. Perhaps if she...

"I'll hire a bathing machine," said Viola.

Polly twisted a corner of her apron.

"Don't go out too deep, Miss. They say the monster comes from the deep."

Sun glinted on the ripples as the water lapped the wheel of the bathing machine. The chain slapped the surface, dipping into each oncoming wavelet. Viola sat on the top step and dipped her naked toe into the water.

A shudder shook the surface. Snippets of excited giggles and splashes snagged in the air. Surely, no one else was foolhardy enough to venture this far from shore?

The faint rumble of an engine surfaced above the slapping of the chains. Viola peeked around the edge of her bathing machine, toward the beach. A second bathing machine halted not far from the shoreline, its distinct red and white stripes standing out against the dark water. Steps led down from the door, facing away from the shore. Steam drizzled from its fluted funnel. A woman in full afternoon dress paced the shoreline, one hand on her head to secure her over-sized sun hat, eyeing the machine's progress. Gears chugged as a concertinaed canvas tent unfolded and kissed the water, providing total privacy for the hidden bather. How daring!

Viola grinned and scanned the dark water around her. Her bathing machine was as far out as the chain mechanism would reach, almost a hundred yards further out to sea than her fellow bather. She was alone.

The smell of sea salt erupted around her with the slap of each wave. Viola eased down the steps and slid her ankle into the depths. She glanced back at the woollen stockings dangling from a wall hook inside the change box and hesitated. If someone should spy her, stocking-less? She was exposed.

There was a faint splash from the bathing machine behind her. She giggled. At least she wasn't naked.

Viola held her breath. The stockings fluttered in the sea breeze. This was a holiday. Time to recuperate. She was supposed to enjoy herself.

She lowered herself onto the next step. Cool liquid caressed her calf - cool and inviting - like easing into a clean silk stocking, lighter than cobwebs. A warm current flowed from the machine's engine and curled around her leg. She let her lungs empty as her muscles relaxed.

The water beckoned, promising to wash away her worries. Viola spread out her arms and leaned forward, letting the water engulf her body, allowing herself to float off the steps. Each wave dissolved haunting memories, even if only for the moment.

She fanned out her arms and rotated her waist, relishing the unrestricted movement free of a controlling corset. She laughed and rolled onto her back, letting the water carry her further from land.

The sun warmed her body. Cool water kissed her neck and face. She licked the salt from her lips and took a deep breath, filling her lungs; her head spun as oxygen rushed to her brain. She skimmed her fingers over the water. *Free.*

A shriek pierced the air. Viola flinched. Brine filled her mouth and rushed up her nostrils. She spluttered, thrust her legs downward into the deep chilly water and kicked to keep her head above water.

Men shouted, their cries unintelligible through water-logged eardrums. The other bathing machine thundered into life. Chains rattled, the engine strained. Frenzied splashes of water accompanied its retreat.

The water trembled around her, pounding on her chest. Viola gasped for air. A new undercurrent tugged at her legs. She rubbed the salt from her eyes and searched the surrounding water. Nothing.

Bubbles tickled her body and erupted on the surface. Something solid grazed her calf. Viola's heart jumped. The Lurker? Goosebumps crawled over her skin.

There's no such thing as monsters.

Water rumbled and churned. Waves sloshed against her torso. She jerked her knees up to her chest, struggling to untangle her limbs from the snarl of the heavy woollen skirt of her bathing costume.

There's no such thing as monsters. There's no such thing as monsters.

Viola shivered. She had drifted further from the bathing machine than she had thought; the candy-striped change box was nearly eighty yards away, the shore even more distant.

A crowd was gathering on the shoreline, waving their arms and shouting.

"Get out of the water!"

Two men swam toward her. Another bathing machine trundled in their wake. The sea hissed. Too close.

Spurts of water burst from the surface. A large shadow lurked beneath her.

Viola's heart raced, her breathing shallow. She wanted to run, to flee, to swim to the safety of the change box, but her arms refused to move.

There's no such thing as monsters.

The shadow turned and glided southward towards the headland. A trace of bubbles marked its course, fading as the shadow disappeared into deeper waters.

The two men splashed closer. Uncomfortably close. Their bare arms glowed white against the dark water.

"Get out of the water!"

Viola spun to face them. The weight of her water-logged pantaloons dragged her downward, slowing her movement. Her skirt swirled up in the current, floating up around her thighs. Balloons of fabric surfaced on the water, leaving her legs exposed...

Viola pulled the skirt below the water, yanking low to cover her legs and cursed under her breath. Big mistake; salty water caught in her throat. She sputtered and caught her breath and swam hastily back to the bathing machine. She dove headlong onto the steps and dragged herself into the change box. The skirt clung to her legs; her loose hair wrapped around her neck like tentacles.

The splashing outside stopped. The walls shook with a thud. Viola jumped, skidded in the growing puddle on the floor. She grabbed the hook, draped with her stockings.

"Are you all right, Miss?" The voice was deep, and close to the doorway.

Viola steadied herself. "Yes, I am well." Her voice was a bit shakier than expected.

"You're not injured?"

"No."

"Did you see it?" asked a second, reedier voice.

"See what?"

"The Lurker? It was right under you." There was a pause. "Did you see the monster, Miss?"

"Shut it, William," replied the deep voice. "We don't want to scare the lassie any more."

There was a shadow on the step.

Viola snatched her robe and flung it around her shoulders. "What monster?" she asked, as she peeked through the doorway.

A tall redheaded man stared back at her. Deep furrows etched his forehead. A sandy-haired man appeared at the bottom step. His eyes widened. His gaze lingered on Viola, tracked down a drenched tendril of hair, fell to the puddle at her stockingless feet, and flicked back to the dark water surrounding the change box. His cheeks reddened.

Viola pulled her robe tight.

"You're a long way from shore, Miss," said the sandy-headed man. "Do you not know of the legend of The Lurker?"

"William!" The redheaded man's deep voice echoed through the change box.

"There's no such thing as monsters." Viola cleared her throat. "It's just a story to titillate the tourists."

"If you say so, Miss." William scoffed. "Come on, Mr Fraser. We know when we're not wanted."

Fraser nudged William and lowered his voice. "Perhaps it is time to return to shore, Miss?"

Viola stared down at the water. Ripples formed a few hundred yards away. Something glinted just above the surface. A dark hump broke the waterline, turned seaward and slipped back under the surface.

Viola nodded.

A cool breeze danced over Viola's cheek, catching a loose wisp of hair. Viola tucked the errant tendril behind her ear and glimpsed the uneaten strawberry tart on the tea tray. Her stomach tightened. She ignored it, poured another cup of tea and sipped the hot liquid. Warmth flooded through her chest and limbs.

The door clicked behind her.

"Tea's always good for shock," said Polly.

"I'm not in shock." Viola swallowed another mouthful of tea. It was

one thing to bathe half-naked, but quite another to be caught at it. What would the locals think of her now? How could she go bathing in public again? Viola felt her cheeks warming and turned toward the window.

"But Miss, you were almost attacked by The Lurker!" Polly placed a plate of biscuits on the tea tray next to Viola. "You promised you wouldn't venture beyond the rocks."

"I did not." Viola placed her cup precisely on its saucer. "Don't be absurd, Polly. We are both rational women, and rational people don't believe in monsters."

The lace curtain flicked the side table. Viola glanced out of the window, toward the open sea. Clouds filled the darkening sky; their shadows crept over the water. Perhaps the shadow was caused by a cloud? Yes, that was it.

"They were chasing shadows," said Viola. But the bubbles? She *hadn't* imagined that. Several other possible explanations already churned in her mind.

Viola raised her skirt above her boot and rubbed her calf. The skin was unblemished but it still stung from the graze. There had to be a rational explanation.

"Perhaps a whale strayed too close?" she whispered. Yes, that was it. She dropped her skirts to the floor. A whale, not a monster.

"Still, perhaps you should keep closer to shore?" Polly tugged at her apron. "...in case of whales."

Viola stood up, crossed to the window and peered out. A constable stood on the beach. A group of men pulled the bathing machines' chains tight and large padlocks slipped through the links. A sandy-haired man separated from the group and looked in her direction. It was the one called William. A cold wave shuddered over Viola's body. She retreated from the window and spun to face to Polly.

"I've decided bathing is not for me." She rubbed her fingers and examined the tips. "It makes my fingers wrinkle like prunes."

Polly's fingers relaxed. "Perhaps a scenic walk, or a visit to the fossil cliffs? I hear you can dig your own dinosaur for a shilling." She scooped up the tea tray. "And if you find a new species, they may name it after you."

Viola's eye widened. "The cliffs to the south, on the headland?"

Polly nodded.

The bubble trail had led south toward the cliffs on the headland. Viola's heart raced. Perhaps she could solve the mystery of the shadow? She snatched up her teacup and quaffed down the dregs.

"Fetch my parasol and field glasses, Polly. I'm going dinosaur hunting."

The wind tugged Viola's skirts. Her parasol dangled from her arm and thumped her thigh with each gust of wind. She peered through her ivory-inlaid field glasses and scanned the, aptly named, Black Sea. Small wavelets rippled across the empty water.

Nothing. No-one dared venture out in a bathing machine, not after yesterday's beastly occurrences, not even after the proprietors had declared there was no charge for the remainder of the week.

Viola flipped a grey tinted lens in front of the eyepiece. The water cleared. The bathing machine's double tracks extended from the concrete wall, where the tethered machines now stood, into the seawater. Her gaze followed the tracks along an outcrop of black rock, spreading like feelers from the yellow cliffs on the headland to the south, to where she had bathed the day before. Still nothing.

She folded the grey lens back into its assembly and peered at the cliffs. A small party of holiday makers had congregated at the base of the cliff, near the far end of the headland, presumably on a paleontological adventure. Two men bent over and pointed at the ground. A woman clung to her hat as she dragged her child away. The shorter man's top hat quivered in the wind and blew away. He yelled and chased it along the ledge. The second man shook his foot and surveyed the open sea. A young couple had broken away from the group and hurried along the headland toward the foreshore.

Viola slipped the field glasses into the lower velvet-lined section of her purse, and secured the clasp. Her lace parasol unfurled with a satisfying click.

"Perhaps I will try some fossil hunting," she said to no-one in particular.

Sand squeaked under Viola's boots. The path led along the foreshore to a small booth nestled against the headland, where the sandstone bluff erupted from the rock and traced the edge of the coastline.

A middle-aged woman grinned at Viola. A fiery mass of curls cascaded onto her shoulders.

"Morning, Miss. Fancy a dig? Find your very own dinosaur bones? No guarantee, of course. Fossils can be fickle. Only a shilling."

Viola delved into her purse, produced a shiny shilling and dropped it into the woman's pudgy fingers.

"Thank 'e, Miss." The coin disappeared. "Just follow the path. Mr Weymess will be available to answer any questions and give assistance if you should need it." She handed Viola a small trowel and pick.

"Thank you." Viola examined the rust-flecked implements and turned toward the path.

Wind gusted as Viola climbed carved steps, leading up to the ledge at the base of the bluff. Gulls cawed as they circled at the end of the headland, drowning out the sound of the waves. A shrill cry pierced the din. Viola halted mid-step. That wasn't a gull.

Hurried footsteps rang on the rock. A raucous sobbing carried on the wind. Viola turned the corner onto the ledge. A teary-eyed debutante dashed toward the steps; her pale-faced beau clutched at her elbow.

"We're off to fetch the Constable," croaked the man. "Best you don't go down there, Miss."

The woman sniffed, her sobs receding as they scampered down the steps toward civilisation.

Viola gripped her parasol and strode forward. She welcomed the prospect of a spot of juicy detectiving to distract her.

Chapter 2:
Dead Man's Shoes

The scene would have been comical, if it had not been for the blood-drenched body. A tall man stood, hands on hips, guarding the crumpled victim. A boy jostled him, in an attempt to spy the corpse. A shorter man furiously fanned a swooning gentlewoman with his top hat, as he rummaged in her purse for smelling salts. Above them circled the lamenting gulls.

Waves lapped over the precipice of the rock ledge, edging closer and soaking into the sandy ground.

Viola straightened her skirts and strode forward.

"Please, Miss." The taller man's moustache twitched as he frowned. "It's no sight for a lady."

Viola collapsed her parasol, hung it on her belt and eyed the well-meaning gentleman. His keen eyes watched everyone. His tweed hiking attire was exceptionally tailored; a pair of field glasses were slung over his shoulder. Perhaps he's a birdwatcher? Well, this would certainly add some excitement to his day.

"I'm trained as a doctor." Viola tugged at the fingertips of her gloves, pulled them off and tucked them into her purse. "I've seen much worse."

He ran his hand over his meticulously trimmed moustache. "I don't think it's a good idea, Miss."

The boy giggled and darted past the man. He spun on his heel, caught the boy's coat and dragged him back.

Viola slipped past him. Her foot sloshed into a large puddle.

"Botheration, my new boots!" Viola stepped back, grabbed her soaked skirts and pulled the hem free of the growing pool of water. She examined the offending puddle; it was half a man's height in diameter. One end fanned out into three projections. It looked like a...

Viola tilted her head to one side and scrutinised the puddle.

"A footprint?" she whispered.

"Pardon, Miss?" said the moustached man.

"I want to see the monster," cried the boy, as he wriggled in his captor's grip.

"Please stand back, Sir," said Viola. "We must preserve all the evidence for the Constabulary." She glanced at the body - a tall man with brown hair. His woollen lounge coat twisted under his body, revealing a blue velvet waistcoat. Blood drenched the material around several deep wounds in his torso.

Viola's heart skipped. He reminded her of Henry. Her stomach tightened. She took a measured breath and steadied herself.

"Does anyone know this poor soul?" she asked.

The woman whimpered behind Viola.

"A Mr Weymess, the overseer of this... paleontological endeavour." The moustached man's voice was concise.

How unfortunate. No chance of obtaining information from him now.

"Is that a footprint?" exclaimed the boy as he squirmed.

The shorter man craned his neck to view the discovery.

"Holy mother of..." He dropped his hat. His companion slumped.

The boy twisted from his captor's grip and fell, his nose gouging the edge of one of the pointed extensions of the footprint.

"It is." He scrambled backwards, slipping in the wet sand. "It's the monster!" He pushed himself to his feet and sped along the path toward the foreshore.

The woman spluttered, pushing her companion's hand from in front of her eyes. She spied the corpse. Her body trembled. A loud wailing followed.

"Who found the body?" asked Viola, as the woman fainted, yet again.

The moustached man jerked his head in the direction of the fainted woman.

Viola crouched next to the puddle and examined it. She dipped her finger into the water and ran it along the floor of the puddle. She frowned. It felt strangely even.

The moustached man squatted beside her. "Shouldn't we wait for the Constable?" he asked.

Viola glanced at the rising tide. Water slapped the precipice of the ledge and cascaded over its edge, moving closer with each wave.

"If he doesn't arrive soon, it will be too late. I don't think we have the luxury of time, do you?"

A foam-edged sheet of water glided closer, rolled over the margin of the footprint and dribbled into the puddle, as if in response.

"At this rate, all the evidence will disappear before the Constabulary rouse themselves." Viola regarded the body behind them. "I doubt if they even have a Police Surgeon to examine those wounds properly."

"You've done this before?" The moustached man eyed Viola.

"Once or twice." Viola stood, dusted the yellow sand from her skirt and turned to the corpse. "See if you can block the tide."

She stepped toward the foot of the corpse and examined the shoes. Dark red-brown clay caked the soles. She plucked a pin from her bun, and scraped some mud from the shoe and wrapped it in a handkerchief.

"But, Miss..." The moustached man hovered a few feet away.

The woman shrieked and fainted, yet again. Her companion groaned and unstoppered the smelling salts for a third time. The moustached man remained silent.

Viola ignored them and continued her examination of the corpse. A small flower was caught around a button on his coat cuff. She plucked it free and studied it; a tubular bulb, less than an inch long, with tufts of light purple woolly bracts.

"Miss, shouldn't you–?" asked the moustached man.

Viola held a finger to her lips to silence him.

Hurried footsteps slapped along the path, followed by a second set with a more plodding gait. The boy skittered around the corner, followed by a constable, and paused near his flustered parents and thrust his finger accusingly in Viola's direction.

"Over there," he spluttered. "He's been eaten by The Lurker."

The Constable surveyed the group; his gaze lingered on the blood-spattered corpse. "Step away from the deceased, please," he said in a clipped voice. "This is police business." He strode up to the corpse and leaned over to examine it. "Did anyone witness the crime?"

Viola shook her head. The moustached man behind Viola stepped forward and cleared his throat.

"And you are?" asked the Constable.

"Mr Peabody. Our dig party come up for a spot of fossicking." Mr Peabody extended his hand in greeting. "But we didn't expect fresh bones."

The Constable glared in his direction.

"And we found the man like this." Mr Peabody dropped his hand.

"How long ago was this?" asked the Constable.

"Almost an hour ago," replied Mr Peabody.

The man with the top hat nodded. The woman whimpered and embraced the boy.

"Look here, my friends are quite upset by all of this. May we leave?" asked Mr Peabody.

The Constable ran his gaze over Mr Peabody and thrust his hands behind his back. "Where are you lodging, sir?"

"The New Inn." replied Mr Peabody.

"Ah, I know the establishment well. Wait by the Weymess' booth until Constable Ridley arrives. He will take down your particulars." The Constable rocked on his heels and sniffed. "You will be required at the Station House first thing in the morning for full statements."

"Of course, Constable," said Mr Peabody.

"And pass on my condolences to Mrs Weymess."

Silver and bronze glinted on Mr Peabody's waistcoat as he tipped his hat in Viola's direction. He moved to aid the flustered trio and ushered the group back toward the path.

The Constable turned his attention to Viola. "And you might be?"

Viola wiped the sand from her hand and thrust it in his direction. She wrapped her fingers around the flower, in her other hand, and buried it in the folds of her skirt.

"Doctor Viola Stewart," she replied.

"Doctor, is it?" The Constable eyed the proffered hand and raised an eyebrow. "And what might you be doing with my body, *Miss* Stewart?"

"Yes, *Doctor*." Viola retracted her hand.

A line of foam oozed into the puddle and rushed back to sea, eroding the footprint. Only a faint outline remained.

"We have our own Surgeon, thank you. But I will require you to give a statement to Constable Ridley."

"As you wish, Constable." Viola nodded and slipped the flower into her hair bun.

The pale, dry sand stretched out before them, like a mummified corpse. Bony fingers of black rock clawed at the retreating water, dug into the sand and reached into the depths of the North Sea. Yellow sandstone erupted from the south flank, rising to form the bluff of the headland.

Viola jumped onto the rock and adjusted the side shields of her tinted spectacles. Polly's worried reflection shimmered in the concealed mirrored prism. She had no doubt Henry had secured Polly's promise to watch over her and ensure she didn't succumb to any folly or detectiving.

She strode along the rock. Her boot heel slipped on the surface. Viola thrust out her arms, using her parasol to regain balance.

"Do be careful, Miss." Polly clutched the picnic basket against her chest. "You don't want to get your new boots soaked again."

Viola straightened her shoulders, determined not to give up on her current quest. The black rock ground underfoot. She edged her way to the end of the outcrop, bent down and ran her fingers over the rough surface. Fine cobwebs of quartz ran through the rock. She rolled the granules in her fingers. It was darker than the particles found on the dead man's shoes. Botheration. She'd have to locate the source of the clay.

She rose slowly and eyed Polly in the side mirror. The furrows etched in her forehead had deepened.

"What is it, Miss?" Polly eyed her through narrowed eyelids.

"Geology is a fascinating subject, don't you think? The rock here is a different colour to that of the headland. Fascinating. I wonder why that is?" Viola dusted her fingers off on her skirt. "Perhaps I should take up the study of geology?"

Polly examined Viola's grey-tinged fingers.

"Perhaps we should return to the beach, Miss?" she replied. "This rock looks too uncomfortable to enjoy your picnic and I'm afraid the ground will dirty your dress."

"There's still time for some more exploring before luncheon, Polly." Viola turned toward the bluff. "And you did insist I get some fresh air."

A breeze tugged at her parasol, as if on cue.

Polly readjusted the basket on her arm, and followed.

The gulls' chorus crescendoed as Viola picked her way to the end of the rock outcrop, to the sea's edge. The formation dipped, creating a steep precipice. The water was dark and deep here, surrounding them on three sides. Waves slapped against the dark rock. The tide was changing.

"Careful, Miss," said Polly. "The locals won't fish here. The boats get pulled down or smash on the rock." Polly lowered her voice. "They say it's The Lurker."

Viola's heart twisted. The scrape on her leg ached. She turned back to face the beach. They had ventured over a hundred yards beyond the shore, almost as far as the end of the headland. She forced a smile.

"Now, Polly, we've discussed this. There is no such thing as a monster."

Movement at the top of the cliff caught her attention. A figure stood near the edge, one hand steadying his hat against the wind. Viola paused mid-step. Someone was watching them.

The figure retreated.

The bluff would give an excellent view of the bay. Perhaps she could track where the bubble-generating shadow had retreated. There's some detectiving to be done up there; but how was she to detach herself from Polly's ever watchful eye?

Another gust of wind tugged at her skirts. Viola tightened her grip on her parasol. The wind caught the silk and jerked it violently. The parasol turned inside out, with a loud rip.

"Botheration." Viola flicked the parasol. The spokes refused to collapse back. Fate had supplied the perfect opportunity to keep Polly busy for the rest of the day. "That was my favourite parasol."

Viola eyed the reflection of the bluff in her side shield. Her foot twitched. "I don't think a beach picnic is a good idea any more, Polly."

Polly's shoulders relaxed. She nodded.

Viola ran her hand along the spine of her frazzled parasol. "I have a mind to do some flower arranging."

"Flower arranging?"

"Yes. A fitting distraction for when one is on holiday, don't you think? And what better than to use native flowers in season?" Viola laughed. "Geology *and* Botany. How civil." She wrapped the parasol's detached trim tight around its exposed ribs. "Polly, did you discover where to find that intriguing foliage?" she asked.

"The Creeping Thistle? Yes, Miss." Polly pointed to the grassy bluff on top of the cliff. "Mrs Weymess said it's found near the old ruins on the bluff. It's easy to spot; nothing likes to grow too close to it." Polly paused and eyed Viola with a sideways glance. "But it's mostly brambles and rock," she said. "Very dangerous, with sink holes and loose rock near the cliff edge."

Viola handed Polly her battered parasol. "Repair the poor thing while I'm away. I'll have tea and scones when I return to the hotel. And some of that delicious blackberry jam."

Polly bobbed in reply.

"Shall I fetch your *visite*, Miss?" she asked. "It will be chilly on the bluff."

"No need. I studied in Edinburgh, remember? The University Halls channelled the arctic chill." Viola laughed. "London hasn't softened me yet." She relieved Polly of the wicker picnic basket, picked up her skirts and strolled back along the outcrop toward the beach. Where had that man gone?

A chill wind buffeted the headland. Grass rolled like waves in a storm, its peaks crashing into each other. Viola steadied her footing on the uneven ground, leaned against the remains of a dry-stone wall near the top of the cliff edge and re-adjusted her tinted spectacles.

She gripped her field glasses and scanned the coastline. The bathing machines stood silent on the beach, their tracks lay abandoned in the

deserted, dark waters.

Viola clicked an auxiliary lens in front of the barrel of her field glasses. A faint outline of a rock reef spread out from the visible outcrops and fell away sharply, just beyond where the tracks ended. Here the water remained dark. There be monsters. Viola swallowed. She hadn't realised how close she'd ventured into the depths. A second lens clicked in place. A darker, convoluted channel wound its way from the sea, along the reef past the bathing machine tracks. Just like the marshes near Cloomber Hall.

It continued past the headland following the direction the unexplained shadow had taken, before it disappeared, leaving only its trail of bubbles. Curiouser and curiouser.

If she moved a little closer to the edge, she could spy past the cliff, beyond the ruined wall. She followed the crumbling dry-stone wall, tracking the cliff edge around the tip of the headland, where it turned south before it disintegrated into clumps of ruins.

The cliff was higher here, offering a full view of the coastline from the beach to the north. The reef spread out below the sandstone bluff, and continued along the cliffs to the southern coastline on the horizon.

A shadow flickered in the corner of Viola's eye. She crouched behind the wall and peeked through a gap between the stones. A figure in a dark hat and flowing Inverness cloak prowled further along the cliff edge, paused near a wall remnant, and looked down at the water. A satchel swung on his shoulder. He adjusted it and continued following the coastline to the south.

Viola narrowed her eyelids. What are you up to?

The stranger clambered onto a mound of stone rubble, surveyed the land to the west, and retreated out of sight.

Twigs wheedled their way into the bows and lace of Viola's bustle skirt. She extracted the annoyances and pulled herself to her feet. The game's afoot! She grinned and made her way through the brambles toward where the stranger had paused to study the water.

The surviving wall remnant was closer to the cliff edge here. Viola inched closer to the precipice for a better vantage point of the water below. What was he looking at? She leaned further forward and peered through her field glasses.

The channel line etched through the water toward the cliff. Rips swirled. Foam-topped waves slapped against the cliff. A cluster of bubbles broke the surface and led away from the sheer cliff of the coastline.

Viola's heart raced as she flipped the auxiliary lens in place. The water cleared, revealing a large oval shadow directly below the bubble trail as it disappeared beneath the overhang.

Where had it gone? She stepped closer to the edge and scanned the rocks below. Nothing. Fine salt spray deposited on her field glasses. Perhaps there was an underground tunnel or a cave? She leaned even further.

Faint splashes caught on the wind. Viola's foot lurched forward. Her toes dipped. Her ankle rolled forward. The ground seemed to sink under her feet. Stones cracked and tumbled, showering onto the rock cliff.

Viola twisted away from the edge, lunged at the wall and grabbed at the protruding rocks of its ruins. Her fingers stung as they scraped on the rough stone and she fell to the ground with a thump.

Stones trickled away from the edge. She scrambled away. Large cracks formed on the precipice. The cracks widened. A chunk of earth dropped, held only by fine roots. It swung in the wind before succumbing to gravity and tumbling into the sea with a loud plop.

Viola's heart pounded. She clung to the wall, struggling to catch her breath and waited for her pulse to slow. Just breathe...

She examined her hands. Beads of blood welled up on her fingertips. Her gloves were shredded. She peeled them off, rolled them up and placed them on her purse. It felt lighter than usual. Viola gasped. Her field glasses!

She searched the ground. They lay at the base of the wall, the ivory-inlay cracked. One of the auxiliary lenses had detached and lay shattered nearby. Her shoulders slumped. She retrieved the field glasses, dusted them off and slipped them into the lower, velvet-lined section of her purse. She sighed. There'd be no more coastal surveillance today.

A hollow tapping sound drifted on the erratic wind, making it impossible to pinpoint its origin.

Viola pulled herself to her feet. Her legs trembled. Her shin ached. She breathed deeply, until her corset tightened and pressed against her lungs. She turned toward the rock mound. Time to find out where he went.

Broken twigs hinted at his progress. Viola followed the meagre trail until she reached the remains of an old stone hut. Weathered signs leaned at irregular angles.

Caution
Danger
Collapsed Rocks

The stone wall was more substantial here, rising half as tall as the hut's wall. She examined the stones. Some areas were less weathered and moss-free, as if partially repaired. But why here? On an abandoned headland? What was he hiding?

Viola followed the wall until she found an opening and climbed over. A small walled yard surrounded the rear of the hut. Tall prickly plants ringed the inside of the fence and spread into the dirt-filled yard. Their spiky leaves grabbed at her skirts and tugged at her sleeve cuffs, catching her buttons.

She carefully plucked the vegetation from her dress and examined one of the tufty lilac-coloured florets. It smelled of honey. Creeping Thistle. She caught her breath. The dead man... He was here.

She scanned the ground and kicked the soil with her toe. A spray of red-brown dirt settled on her boot. She pulled a handkerchief from her purse, wiped the soil off and examined the particles. They were the same as those on the dead man's shoes. He had definitely been here. But why?

Viola folded up the handkerchief and tucked it into her purse. She searched the yard. Nothing. She searched the wall, the thistle hedge.

"There's nothing here!" She reached down to remove some brambles from her stockings.

Faint footprints led through a stand of creeping thistle and into the stone hut. Viola wrapped her skirt around her hand and pushed aside the brambles. Inside was nothing but rubble. She lifted her tinted spectacles and waited for her eye to adjust to the shadows. The far wall seemed more substantial than the rest; the rubble seemed to have been cleared from the area. She squeezed past the thistles. Her feet thudded on the earthen floor as she kicked stones clear and pushed debris aside with her foot. What was so special about–?

Viola's boot clanged. She froze. She tapped her toe on the ground.

Clang. What was he hiding?

The ground had been disturbed; scrape marks led to where Viola stood. She felt the ground. Cold. Hard. There was a lip, an edge. She traced her fingers along it until she found a chink. She poked her fingers into the hole and explored the area. There was a circular button. She pressed it.

The ground hissed and shook under her feet. Viola jumped off the hatch, as it lowered slowly into the darkness. A warm current floated up through the hole.

Viola removed her spectacles, tightened her eye patch and peered into the depths. A faint breeze fluttered across her face, carrying the smell of brine and old fish. Her nose wrinkled.

A rusty ladder was bolted to the side of the shaft. She reached into her purse for her gloves. Gone. She must have lost them somewhere on the bluff while searching for her field glasses. She eyed the grimy rungs. Her mind returned to Arthur's book. Was the stranger like the monks in *Cloomber Hall*? Was *he* leading her into a bottomless pit?

Viola took a deep breath. She had no choice. She had to investigate. She gathered up her skirts, tucked them in to her belt and stepped into the hole.

Chapter 3: Into the Depths

The smell of fish and seaweed permeated the shaft. Viola buried her nose in her sleeve and breathed through her mouth. The dank air thickened as she descended into the unlit depths. Chill crept into her bones. She stared into the darkness. How deep did it go? Had she been lured into a bottomless pit, just like General Heatherstone? Was the figure a real-life mysterious monk, like in the book?

She eased down, her toes feeling for the next rung. The metal clanked. Flecks of rust embedded themselves in the grazes in her fingers and palms, and crumbled, showering down from the rung above, settling on her eyelashes. She winced.

Something rattled in the dark. She froze, one foot in mid-air, and held her breath. The sunlight from the entrance didn't penetrate this far; there was no way of telling how close, or what, it was. She tightened her grip and turned her ear toward the sound. Why hadn't she packed her night goggles?

A faint scrape. A scuffle. Viola's lungs complained. Her fingers burned. Knuckles cramped. She couldn't hang off the side of the shaft forever.

Her lungs spasmed as she resisted the urge to empty her stomach of its contents. She gulped in a mouthful of foul air.

The shaft remained silent.

She lowered her foot and probed for the next rung. Her foot thudded on earth. At last. She stretched out her hand and clawed at the air. Her fingers rammed into something hard. Something heavy. Metal rattled. Something... movable.

Viola ran her fingers along a linked chain. It emerged from a box with dull-edged cogs. Where was she? She peered into the darkness. A cave?

A faint light flickered in the distance. Lines emerged from the darkness. An oily mechanical contraption squatted in the corner of an alcove adjacent to the shaft. Several chains rose from its carcass, passing through a lifting platform, and led up to a pulley system. It reminded Viola of the ascension chamber used to deliver equipment down to her laboratory. The lifting platform seemed just large enough to fill the shaft. She looked up toward the entrance; the chains rose the entire height of the shaft, to a pulley hidden under the open hatch.

The light flickered and brightened, outlining a tunnel leading from the alcove into a small subterranean grotto. Footprints trailed out of the alcove and into an adjoining area filled with tarpaulin-covered crates.

Clunk.

Something shuddered further down the tunnel. Viola ducked behind the lifting contraption.

Clunk.

She peered into the deep shadows. The tunnel led east, toward the coast... toward where she had seen the bubbling shadow disappear into the cliff.

Was this the Lurker's lair? She shrank behind the lifting platform and gripped one of the chains. It couldn't be.

Clank.

Chugging echoed along the tunnel. Muffled voices drifted in her direction.

A mechanical? Viola's grip relaxed. Of course! She should never have listened to Polly's flights of fancy. There are no such things as monsters.

Light crept along the tunnel and spilled into the grotto. Viola retreated into the adjacent alcove, concealed herself behind the crates and waited.

The chugging faltered and gurgled to a halt. She peered into the tunnel. Long shadows crept closer.

Viola nestled into the copious folds of dusty canvas.

"I favour surveillance over heroics, don't you?" The voice was calm. Warm breath caressed her ear.

Viola gasped, jerked her head away from the voice and jumped clear of the tarpaulin. A flash of silver caught her eye. A gentle hand clasped over her mouth.

"Shh, you don't want the monster to hear you," whispered the voice.

"The only monsters down here are men," Viola mumbled.

"The worst kind of monster." The figure remained hidden in the shadows. "Tell me the truth; are you in league with these villains?"

Viola shook her head.

"Then I apologise for the restraint, Miss, but surveillance, by definition, should be covert; I must ask you not to scream and give away our position."

Viola nodded.

He peeled his hand away from her mouth.

Viola glared at the stranger; a dark bowler sat low on his forehead, a tweed Inverness coat draped over his shoulders. A finely-tailored, and familiar, red waistcoat hugged his chest.

"Mr Peabody? What are you doing here?"

"I do apologise but one can't be too careful in my business." He pulled a small tube from his satchel, extended it, rested it over the top of a crate and squinted into the eyepiece.

"What–?" whispered Viola.

"I wasn't expecting company down here." Mr Peabody turned and eyed her up and down. "And what would a respectable lady, such as yourself, be doing skulking around down here, with the likes of me?"

"I wasn't skulking." Viola felt her cheeks burn. "And I asked you first."

The mechanical in the tunnel clattered and sputtered.

Viola flinched, tripped over a wayward piece of tarpaulin and lost her balance. A strong arm wrapped around her waist. She could feel his chest rise and fall, in time with his breath on her neck. The heat from her cheeks crept down her neck.

"I believe we have not been introduced properly, Mr Peabody," she said.

"I am at a disadvantage, Miss. You know my name, but I do not know yours," he whispered.

"Doctor Viola Stewart." She tried to lean forward.

"Doctor?" Mr Peabody relaxed his grip, but did not relinquish his gentle hold.

"Yes."

"I didn't realise any woman had been..."

"Trained as a doctor?" Viola cleared her throat. "Yes, but not permitted to practice. Current vocation: optician. In London." Viola shifted her weight to increase the distance between them. "I work as consultant for the Marylebone Police, on occasion. Their surgeon is a close friend."

Mr Peabody's arm slipped from her waist. He rocked back on his heels. "Yes. The Marylebone Police assisted in the Whitechapel Murders investigation. I know the case. I believe some unlicensed mechanicals were involved?" His gaze fell on Viola's eyepatch. His eyes widened. "You must be the one-eyed scientist?"

"The–?" Viola glared at him.

"Your reputation precedes you," he replied.

"Sir, if you think your flattery will excuse your behaviour, then–"

"I meant no disrespect." His moustache drooped. "It's just... I assumed you would have been..."

"A man?" Viola's fingers dug into her palms.

Mr Peabody rubbed his fingers along his moustache and pinched his chin.

"Taller." He raised his scope and scanned the tunnel. His hat had been knocked in the scuffle and now sat at a precarious angle. A dark fringe fell over his forehead. He smelt of new leather and spices.

Viola twisted the ring on her left hand. How much did he know?

"How do you know about the mechanicals?" she asked. "It wasn't in the papers. Scotland Yard made sure of that."

"That is..." Mr Peabody continued to survey the tunnel. "...privileged information."

"What do you mean: privileged?"

"Doctor Stewart, my work relies on secrecy. I cannot inform you of its nature," he replied.

Viola puffed her cheeks. How rude! He had lured her into a dark pit and hadn't the courtesy to explain why. She grasped his arm and turned him to face her.

"That is not an acceptable answer. As you said before: You know my vocation. Please give me the courtesy of knowing yours."

"I believe I was discussing names, not vocations."

"In view of our situation, I deserve to know what danger it presents."

He turned the end of the scope.

"You owe me at least that much." Viola pulled back her hand. The lace of her cuff snagged on a button of his coat and tugged it open. Botheration.

Mr Peabody lowered the scope and sighed. He lifted his coat and unhooked the lace strand by strand. A round badge of silver and brass glinted in the low light.

Viola gasped and jerked her sleeve free, with a rip. "No!" He was one of *them*.

He frowned and tilted his head to one side. "What did I do?" he whispered.

"Keep away from me, you're a–" She scrambled away and glanced at the badge on his waistcoat: a silver lightning bolt overlaid on a brass cog. She paused. Not a Man in Grey? Her foot slipped in the dirt as she peered at the badge.

"Your badge... It's the same as the corpse we found near the bluff."

Mr Peabody looked directly into her eye. "That *corpse* was my friend."

Viola straightened her shoulders and stared back: "Who *are* you?"

Mr Peabody straightened his coat. "I must apologise, again. I was under the misapprehension that you were part of the smuggling ring we've been investigating and assumed you were an accomplice to my friend's murder."

Viola's body tensed. "I would never–?"

He held up a calming hand. "I admit my mistake. I now realise you were conducting an investigation."

Viola relaxed.

"Did Scotland Yard have you sign papers?" he asked.

Viola nodded slowly. She had no choice. *For the sake of the Empire,* they'd said.

"Then, it seems we have both been working under mistaken assumptions. It seems formal introductions are in order." He wiped his hands on his trousers and proffered his right hand. "I am Mr Wood, of the Department of Curiosities. That corpse was my fellow operative, Mr Cooper. He was a good friend, a daemon at chess and a jolly-good bridge player."

"You're not Mr Peabody then?"

"No. That was a ruse. The Department prefers to keep its investigation secret."

"Is Wood your real name?"

Mr Wood smiled and reset the scope back on the box and peered through the eyepiece.

Viola raised an eyebrow. "The Department of...?"

"... Curiosities."

"Never heard of it."

"I expect not. It's best not to attract attention. All hush-hush, for the good of the Empire."

"And you catch smugglers?" Viola eyed him through slitted lids. "Why would the Queen concern herself with such trivialities?"

"Only when they smuggle illegal mechanicals in from Europe," he replied.

"Mechanicals?" Viola's breath quickened.

"Dangerous ones. It's our task to find them, stop them and acquire the contraband."

"So you can study and improve on them?" asked Viola.

He glanced at her and shook his head.

"So we can catalogue and store them," he replied.

"To what purpose?" Viola crept closer.

"To no purpose," he replied, "until The Crown decides otherwise. We can't have un-authorised mechanicals let loose on the masses. It would endanger the Empire."

"But they could improve so many lives. If you explained–?"

Mr Wood lowered his scope and turned to Viola. Deep furrows etched his brow.

"Those papers you signed," he said. "The Department is covered by the same Act. You are bound by secrecy, with regards to this entire affair, including the mechanical. Or risk prosecution for treason."

Treason? Viola plopped down on the earth. But why would Her Majesty not wish the lives of her subjects to be improved by such advancements?

Viola ran her gaze over the crates. Several wooden boards had been removed, revealing gadgets of various sizes: a large metal box adorned with glass tubes and brass piping, and jars of curled wire. She lifted the corner of the closest tarpaulin. A small, wheeled, half-spherical contraption fell onto the earth.

"How adorable." She scooped up the device and ran her fingers over the smooth metal. Small wheels poked out from the bottom. Between them was a dial, two buttons and a metal switch. She pressed one of the buttons. The top popped open, revealing a small recessed compartment. Viola poked her fingers inside the cavity. The device was hollow.

Mr Wood cleared his throat and lifted the device from her palm, snapped the compartment shut and pushed it back into the crate.

"That adorable Bot was designed to deliver a bomb. It can find its way through a maze of buildings or rooms, and detonate only when it has found its target."

"Oh?"

"Best not to touch anything else," he replied.

Viola wiped her hand on her skirt, not taking her eye off the Bot. It could also be used to convey messages, deliver food. If she inserted a small camera... "But–?"

The machinery in the tunnel clattered and chugged back into life, filling the cave with an erratic hum. Steam belched and hissed out of the tunnel and into the alcove. A rhythmic click-clack inched closer.

A glow pierced the smoke, now engulfing the entire tunnel.

Mr Wood clasped Viola's wrist. "No time for that now," he said. "We've got company."

Shadows formed in the smoke.

Viola shuffled closer to the end of the crate barricade and peeked around the edge. A waggon trundled into the grotto, trailing smoke from its metal flue. Its contents were hidden by a sailcloth. One corner flapped tantalisingly in time with the vibrating engine.

Viola's pulse raced. "What's the plan?" she whispered.

Mr Wood tugged gently on her wrist. His hand slipped into her gloveless palm. Viola's breaths quickened. Her ears tingled.

He turned her to face him. "You stay here."

"But there's at least two of them." Viola removed her hand. "And you are a man down."

"I'm not authorised to enlist civilians." He snapped the scope shut and shoved it into his satchel. Mr Wood's moustache twitched. He glanced at the waggon and back to Viola, and sighed. "Very well, but you must do exactly as I say."

Viola bit her lip, trying not to grin.

"Is that understood?" he said.

Viola nodded.

"I'll deal with the villains," he instructed as he rummaged in his satchel. "You ascertain the contents of that waggon."

"Do you have a gun?" asked Viola.

Mr Wood glared at her. "We are not uncivilised, Doctor Stewart." He retrieved a hand-sized glass canister from his satchel, with a screw-on metal nozzle and balloon-pump at one end, and unwrapped its rubber tube and handed it to her. A pale-green liquid sloshed in the canister.

"Perfume?"

Mr Wood shook his head, pulled out a second canister from the satchel and unwound the rubber tube. "It's an Incapacitating Liquid Nebuliser. Spray this directly at your opponent and he is rendered unconscious."

Viola sniffed the nozzle and recoiled. A faint, pungently-sweet odour filled her nostrils. Pain shot through her right eye socket. She knew that smell all too well.

"Chloroform." Viola's head ached. She held the canister at arm's length. "And ether?"

Mr Wood smiled. "With a few additions."

"May I ask what additions?" The contents felt cool against her bare palm.

"Just don't drop it," he replied as he edged past the end crate. "Only use it if one of them gets too close." He turned and looked her in the eye. "And try not to breathe it in."

Viola swallowed. If only she hadn't lost her gloves. She ducked back behind the crates; her purse thumped the wood. The Bots rattled.

She sucked in a quick breath. The things she could do with them... Surely, he wouldn't mind, just one...? She glanced back at her newly acquired colleague. He was otherwise engaged with preparing an ambush for the oncoming felons. She wrapped her fingers around one of the Bots, extracted it from the crate and slipped it into one of the pockets hidden under her bustle.

Loud footsteps thudded along the tunnel. Mr Wood froze. Viola grabbed her Nebuliser and crouched behind the barricade, ready for action.

The wooden waggon broke clear of the smoke and rattled along a length of track toward the alcove, stopping a few feet inside the cave mouth. Two burly men lumbered out of the tunnel behind it.

Mr Wood tumbled back behind the crate and slid towards Viola. His hat skittered into the shadows. She slammed her back into the crates. The Bot poked deep into her hip. She bit her tongue. Botheration. She hoped it wasn't damaged.

Mr Wood twisted his body, rolled onto his feet and snatched up his hat. "My apologies, Doctor."

"Apologies accepted, Mr Wood." Viola straightened her shoulders and peered over the crates. Two men stood by the waggon, gesticulating wildly, their animated conversation muffled by the chugging of the engines, apparently oblivious to the movement in the storage alcove.

"What do we do now?" she asked.

"We need to examine the contents of that waggon." He checked his Nebuliser. "We need a distraction."

The taller smuggler shouted instructions as he pulled a long lever on the side of the waggon. It hissed and shuddered. A cloud of grey smoke burst from the waggon and engulfed them.

Perfect timing. "Like that?" Viola rose to her feet and hefted the canister in one hand.

Mr Wood stood up beside her. "Exactly like that." His moustache flicked up at each end. "You take the one on the right. And don't aim that thing in my direction." he replied as he disappeared into the growing cloud.

Viola took a deep breath and followed Mr Wood into the haze.

Heat rolled over Viola's skin. Beads of sweat rolled down her forehead. Steam burned her throat. Her eyes watered as they searched the cloud for a target.

A sudden jab sent her reeling backward into the waggon. Its lever sunk into her back, forcing the air from her lungs. She spluttered and struggled to regain her breath. The smell of burning silk mingled with the all-pervading smell of fish.

Viola clasped the ball-plunger in her hand, thrust the Incapacitating Liquid Nebuliser in front of her and searched for any sign of movement in the thinning vapour.

A shadow moved toward her.

Viola held her breath, closed her eye and squeezed the ball-plunger.

"Bloody hell!" The gruff voice echoed in the grotto. The shadow retreated. A faint scuffle broke the silence, followed by a satisfying thud.

Where did he go? She batted away wisps of steam. The smuggler lay crumpled before her, his cheeks fluttering as he snored.

Viola grinned and spun toward the waggon. The shorter smuggler thudded to the ground at her feet.

Mr Wood emerged from the remaining cloud. Wisps clung to his body. Blood dripped from his arm.

"You're hurt," gasped Viola.

"Nothing serious." He kicked the smuggler's dropped knife out of reach. "What's in the waggon?"

Viola tucked up her skirts, stepped over the body and lifted the canvas.

Mr Wood wrapped the rubber tube around his Nebuliser canister, slipped it back into his satchel and joined her. A polished mahogany box sat in one of the crates. He ran his hand over one of the three etched-brass tubes snuggled in padded velvet beside it.

"Excellent. A Matter Re-Imager. We'd had word there may be one in this shipment." He lifted the box and grinned. "We couldn't allow it to fall into The Society's hands."

Viola's eye widened. A Magic Lantern. She stepped away from the waggon, nudging the smuggler's body with her foot.

"You know of The Society?" asked Mr Wood.

Viola nodded, her gaze locked on the crate's contents.

"No need to worry, Doctor Stewart, we've foiled whatever devious scheme they had in mind for it."

"They've already got one," she whispered. She kicked away the smuggler's hand.

"That's impossible." Mr Wood narrowed his eyes. "How do you know that?"

"I've had the displeasure of seeing a demonstration first hand." She backed away further, trying to step around the smuggler's snoring lump.

"Really?" Mr Wood raised an eyebrow. "That's not in your file."

"I suspect there's a lot of things not in my file, Mr Wood."

"You'd be surprised, Doctor Stewart." His moustache twitched. "We must talk about automatons some time."

Viola's skin crawled. She was usually the one doing the detectiving. It hadn't occurred to her that someone could be watching back.

"The Department of Curiosities, you say?" She took another step. "Or spies? What do you really do, Mr Wood?"

Mr Wood eased the box back into the crate. "We ensure the safety of the Empire, Doctor Stewart." His hand plunged into his satchel.

Was this Department thing just another ruse? Viola's finger wrapped around the rubber plunger of her Nebuliser. Or was he in league with the smugglers all along? "And does that require poking into people's personal–?"

A rough hand latched onto her leg, dragging her skirt. Viola shrieked.

"How–?" Mr Woods raised his Nebuliser and scowled.

Another hand grabbed at her waist. The Nebuliser was knocked from her hand and skittered into the tracks near the waggon. Glass smashed. Liquid sizzled.

"Larger doses are required for increased body mass," replied Viola. "Anaesthesiology is not an exact science." She struggled to keep her balance as the smuggler dragged at her waist and pulled himself up from the ground. His other hand clasped over her mouth. "I miscalculated," she mumbled.

Mr Wood's gaze darted in the direction of the waggon, before settling on Viola's assailant. He aimed the Nebuliser in her direction.

Viola struggled to escape her captor's grip. She didn't trust Wood not to incapacitate them both and leave her behind. She swallowed. This time there was no Henry to swoop to her aid, even belatedly. She was on her own. She closed her eye, parted her lips and sank her teeth into the sooty flesh of the smuggler's hand.

The smuggler howled and shoved her away. He lurched backwards, flicking his hand and cursing. Droplets of blood spotted on her bodice.

She fell forward, catching the edge of the waggon. A pungent, sweet odour warmed her lungs. Her head spun.

Mr Wood surged forward. Bursts of fine mist filled the air, settling on the smuggler's face. His eyes rolled upward, until they were nothing but white orbs. He hovered, then wobbled and slumped to the floor.

"Was that enough?" asked Mr Wood.

A wave of nausea rolled over Viola. She struggled to focus. "Botheration." Her words slurred. Not again. She ripped the ruffle from her hem and wrapped it around her mouth and nose.

Mr Wood's face shimmered before her. Her body shuddered as another wave of nausea swept through her. Her feet lifted off the floor. The grotto spun in a flurry of flame and steam.

Water lapped near Viola's head. She felt hard ground against her back. Cold seeped through her bodice. She opened her eye and scanned the dim chamber. A figure stood, silhouetted by a flickering glow in the tunnel beyond. It stepped forward and hesitated.

Popping noises bounced along the tunnel.

Viola drew in a deep breath of salty air. Her chest shuddered. Her head began to clear. She rolled to face the figure, sat up - ever so slowly - and ventured another breath. The air smelled of wood smoke. Tendrils of dark smoke crawled along the roof of the tunnel.

Mr Wood turned, his hands clenched. His gaze settled on Viola.

"Such a shame to lose the Matter Re-Imager." He helped Viola to her feet. "Ever ridden in a submersible?"

Viola sucked in an excited breath. Another cough shuddered through her body. "No."

She stood on the edge of an underground pool. To one side, a scaffolding supported a network of chains and pulleys leading to a large crank. Water lapped an oval-shaped submersible as big as three carriages. Six large, segmented appendages emerged from the lower half of the wood and metal hull, piercing the water below.

The far end of the submersible was a dome of glass, encased in a bronze cage. A lantern dangled in front of the dome, from a jointed arm at the top of the hull. Its eerie green glow reflected in the ripples of water as they lapped the submersible.

Viola's heart fluttered. A submersible! She'd heard stories, but never dreamed she would actually see one.

"The Lurker?" she whispered.

Mr Wood adjusted his newly stuffed satchel and nodded. "No time to dally." He bowed and gestured toward the wooden ramp leading up to the submersible. "After you, Doctor Stewart."

A sputtering roar rumbled along the tunnel toward them.

Viola flinched and hurried along the ramp. Her boots clanked on the metal rungs on the side of the hull, leading up to a hatch. She spun the wheel. The hatch sprung open.

Black smoke belched from the tunnel.

Viola lowered herself into the belly of the submersible. Green light flickered to life inside. A spiral staircase descended.

Copper and bronze glimmered around her. Dials and gauges dominated one wall. Brass tubing ran along the opposite wall and curved down into the floor in front of a brass trellis separating the back half of the cabin from the main area. A raised panel of switches and buttons sat between two padded, green armchairs, facing the glass dome. Double-handled levers rose from the floor, one in front of each chair.

Viola's eye widened. It was just like a motorwagon.

The hatch clanged shut. Mr Wood hurried past her, plopped into one of the chairs and lowered the leather harness over his shoulders. He studied the console, took a deep breath and flicked a switch.

"You'd better sit down," he said.

"You know how to operate a submersible?" asked Viola as she slipped into the right hand chair and buckled the straps over her chest.

"I've studied the plans of a similar mechanical." He wrapped his hands around the handles on either side of his steering lever. "It's a bit like riding a plectocycle." He winked and nudged the lever forward.

The submersible lurched. A metal appendage glided past the glass and plopped into the water in front of the dome. Viola's stomach churned. He pushed the lever further forward. The submersible lurched again. She held her stomach and breathed slow, deep breaths.

"Are we going to walk all the way home?" she asked.

Mr Wood shook his head and flicked another switch. The submersible wobbled, lowered into the water and floated forward. He pulled back on both levers. Bubbles rushed past the dome; it surged forward along an underwater channel and into open water.

Butterflies somersaulted in Viola's stomach. She glanced behind them. "It's a shame to leave all those magnificent mechanicals behind."

"Better destroyed than in the possession of unauthorised individuals or The Society."

"Perhaps some survived?" she said, already formulating a plan to return. "The smoke will clear in a day or so."

Mr Wood smiled.

"But everything will be recovered and catalogued by then," he said.

"For the good of the Empire?" Viola's shoulders slumped.

"For the good of the Empire," replied Mr Wood. "Where to next, Doctor Stewart?"

Viola straightened her skirts. "Polly will be waiting with scones and blackberry jam." Her fingers knocked the hidden Bot in her pocket. The corner of her lip quivered. She bit her lip, stifling a grin, stared out of the dome window and patted her pocket.

THE END

Tomorrow, When I Die

Chapter 1:
The Chronic Argonauts

The midday sun streamed across the kitchen table. Viola plunged the wooden spoon into the pudding bowl, with a satisfying squelch. She licked her lips and stirred the thick mixture.

Bowls clattered behind her. Polly hummed quietly. Viola closed her eye and smiled. It was the same tune her mother used to hum.

"Oh, why can't we have Christmas more often?" She plopped another sixpence into the mixture.

Polly raised an eyebrow. "Isn't one sixpence more traditional?"

"Sir Archibald will be disappointed if he misses out again this year." Viola inhaled the sweet smell of candied orange peel, currants and brown sugar. She dunked her finger into the concoction and licked her fingertip. "A little more nutmeg, I think?"

Polly dipped a teaspoon into the spice tin and dusted nutmeg over the fruit mixture. She scooped the pudding onto the cloth, gathered up the corners and knotted them.

"Will Doctor Collins will be well enough to join you for Christmas Eve?" Polly slipped the parcel onto a wooden dowel and lowered it into a pot of boiling water. "It's been weeks since the accident."

"He's lucky he didn't shatter the bone," replied Viola. Taking irrational and unnecessary risks. Again. She'd had everything under control until Henry decided she needed rescuing. Her heart ached. *He could have died!*

Polly frowned.

"Sir Archibald has ordered him to rest up until Lady Calthorpe's party," said Viola. "He's engineered a contraption to help with manoeuvrability." Shadows across the table faded as grey clouds crept across the sky. "Looks like rain."

"And the forecast had been for fine weather for the party." Polly sighed. "I do hope it doesn't spoil afternoon tea with Doctor Collins."

"He'll cope until the festivities tomorrow night." Viola flexed her fingers. "He's driving me to distraction. Every afternoon, the same questions. He wants to know every detail about my day."

"He is very fond of you, Miss." Polly's cheeks flushed.

Viola gazed out of the kitchen window and tracked the clouds as they blocked the sun. *He's worried I'll go off on an adventure without him. Why can't he trust me?* She clenched her hands. *I suspect he has Sir Archibald keeping watch on me.*

"Am I not as able as any man?" she whispered. *Perhaps she should go on an adventure, by herself, just to show him?*

Polly cleared her throat. "He is fortunate you were there, Miss."

Viola picked up a stray currant from the bench and popped it in her mouth.

"I'll only want a light supper tonight, Polly. I think I'll settle in with a good book after I return from afternoon tea."

"A new Sherlock Holmes?" Polly's eyes lit up.

"No," replied Viola. "Sir Archibald has promised me something new this afternoon. Doctor Doyle calls it science fantasy. It's a fantastical tale about a man in search of his true time."

A loud pounding echoed down the hall from the front doorway. Viola glanced at the small clock on the wall. Two o'clock.

"Are you expecting any visitors, Miss?" Polly dusted her floury hands on her apron and yanked it off.

Viola shook her head, arranged her skirts and followed Polly into the entry hall. Polly straightened her cap and opened the door.

Sir Archibald bustled into the hall, his cheeks flushed. His gaze darted along the hall until he spotted Viola. His spectacles jiggled precariously on the tip of his nose as he puffed. Polly stepped back and caught his coat and cane as he tossed them aside.

"Has something happened?" Viola's heart sank. "Is it Henry?"

Sir Archibald shook his head and caught his breath.

"Polly, get Sir Archibald a brandy."

Polly bobbed and skittered down the hall.

"What's happened, Sir Archibald?" Viola placed her hand on his shoulder.

"It's... I've been... oh, God." Deep furrows etched his forehead; he leaned against the wall. "Viola, you must help me." He looked her in the eye. "Tomorrow, I'm going to die."

Viola observed Sir Archibald as she wrapped a blanket around his shoulders. The soles of his shoes were scuffed, the cuff of his trousers torn. His face was still pale and his gaze darted around the room, lingering on the door and window, never meeting Viola's eye.

"You've had enough brandy," she said.

"What would you do?" he mumbled. "If the fate of the Empire rested on it?"

Viola frowned and added four spoons of sugar to his drink. "Drink your tea. It will clear your head."

"I don't want to die." Sir Archibald's tea cup rattled on its saucer. He clenched his hands but still they trembled. "But if it's for the good of the Empire...?" His hand clasped his inside jacket pocket.

"You can't possibly know you will die tomorrow," said Viola. His mind was still muddled. She placed her palm on his forehead. No fever. "How long were you wandering about last night?" She checked his pulse.

"I've seen the future, Viola."

Viola shook her head. *Impossible.*

"It's like the Chronic Argonaut." Sir Archibald gulped his tea.

"The–?"

"That story by the school teacher. I was going to give you a copy this afternoon." He removed Viola's hand from his wrist. "Do you believe in travelling through time?"

Viola's eye widened. "Surely the science is unachievable?"

"There was a closed lecture on temporal displacement, by a Professor Black, at one of the regular Research Meetings," replied Sir Archibald.

"But the amount of energy required would be astronomical. The cost alone would be prohibitive."

"I have irrefutable proof. I wasn't supposed to bring anything back with me." He leaned forward clutching at his jacket. "Too dangerous. Could change everything. But I had to."

A corner of crumpled paper peeked out from under his jacket. Viola seized the folded paper and flipped it open.

THE TIMES
24th December, 1889.
Queen's Traitor Physician Shot Dead After Assassinating Queen.
Sir Archibald Huntington-Smythe, prominent biomechanical surgeon and personal physician to Her Majesty betrays sacred trust.

"But that's impossible."

"Just improbable." Sir Archibald snatched back the newspaper and shoved it in his pocket. "But, I assure you, it is real."

"But..." She sat down beside him. "Surely there's been a

misunderstanding? Perhaps if you return the newspaper, change your actions? That would create an alternate future and avoid–?"

"No." Sir Archibald shook his head. "I cannot go back, or forward, to mend my mistakes. Professor Black won't let me travel again."

"Then what is the point of knowing such events if one can't change them?" asked Viola.

"The Professor said he could help. He is expecting me tomorrow. I wandered all night, trying to think of another way." Sir Archibald pushed his spectacles up his nose. "He requires information about The Queen. Private things. Things covered by the Secrets Act. But I can't... How can I trust them? I can't tell them..." He swallowed and spoke quickly. "Better to die than be branded a traitor."

"You're not a traitor."

"And therefore I must die tomorrow. Unless..." A faint smile flickered over his lips. "That is why I am here." He clasped Viola's hand in his. "I need your help."

Viola raised an eyebrow.

"We can prevent it," said Sir Archibald. "Perhaps, if you can find the true traitor, and prove who is behind the assassination? I won't need to die or, if it is still my fate, then it will not be for nothing."

"Does Henry know?" she asked. He was Sir Archibald's best friend. Surely he would help?

"No, he can barely walk without assistance." Sir Archibald shook his head. "And I don't trust anyone's detectiving but yours. You must travel in my place. Only you could solve this conundrum, Viola."

Viola shifted in her chair. It seemed simple enough. At its heart, it was a causality logic puzzle, but with the added complication of time travel. She smiled. And she was unknown to the Professor, so he wouldn't suspect her of subterfuge. Except... Her shoulders slumped.

"But they will recognise this." Her fingers skimmed over her eye patch. "All of West London knows of the 'one-eyed doctor'."

Sir Archibald smiled. "I've thought of that. How do you feel about disguises?" he asked.

"Disguises?"

"Professor Marchland, one of the Research Meeting fraternity, died last month in a laboratory accident. It was he who introduced me to Professor Black and his temporal machine. I may have mentioned his sister, and research partner, had returned from the continent to sort out his estate. They've never met her." He turned his tea cup on the saucer. "Professor Marchland wished to bequeath money to a worthy research cause. And Professor Black is in need of funds for further research." He grinned. "They are expecting her tomorrow at three o'clock."

"She helped in his research?"

Sir Archibald nodded.

"I can wear my tinted spectacles." Viola sat on the edge of her seat. "I could say I was injured in the accident, damaged my eyes, and have photophobia." Yes, that could work.

"Excellent." Sir Archibald sipped his tea. "Then it's settled. There's a vacant house across the street. I'll wait there until you return."

"No," said Viola. "We need to keep you safe. You must stay here. I insist. Then afternoon tea with Henry. All will be well."

"But you can't go alone–"

"What choice do you have?" asked Viola. "Trust me, Sir Archibald. You shall be partying tomorrow night with the rest of us."

Viola's taffeta hem rustled against the steps as she approached the door. She lifted her ebony skirts and winced. It had been three years since she had abandoned the trappings of mourning. She'd not expected to be wearing black again so soon. Donell had preferred her in blue - the colour of fresh water under a clear sky. She paused on the top step. He'd

promised to take her to Venice before...

Viola tugged at the high collar. It was tighter than she remembered. She took a deep breath, letting the cool air spread into her lungs.

...before Anne abandoned her. Viola released her grip on her skirts and adjusted her tinted spectacles. This was a ruse; it wasn't real.

Her skirts swished as she turned to face number twenty-three Stanhope Street. Faint cracks lined the fading paint of the front door. Her smudged reflection drifted across the dull knocker. It was in dire need of a good spit and polish. Viola examined its face; the lion's head was loose, tilting slightly to the left. No wonder Professor Black was in need of more funds to fill the coffers. It seemed he preferred to spend money on inventions than on the upkeep of his house.

Viola glanced along the line of unkempt houses with bedraggled curtains or boarded up windows. The entire street seemed to need attention, making the Professor's house, and that of his two neighbours, seem almost stately. She raised her hand to the knocker.

The door opened.

A middle-aged footman with greying hair and watchful eyes stared back at her.

Viola lowered her hand. "I've an appointment to see Professor–"

"Good afternoon, Miss Marchland." He nodded and stepped aside. "Sir is expecting you."

Viola entered the hall.

"I am very early. I do hope I've not inconvenienced Professor Black?"

The footman clicked the door closed.

"Time is irrelevant."

He led the way along the hall, past a curiosity cabinet filled with exquisite oddities, past an ornately painted Oriental vase on the hall table, past the dining room. Crockery rattled as a maid cleared the table after luncheon. The footman continued to the end of the hall and halted in front of a closed door.

"Sir requested you join him in the laboratory."

The door squeaked open. A round-faced man with wiry mutton chop sideburns smiled; his narrow bow tie quivered as he nodded. "Welcome, Miss Marchland."

An antique grandfather clock clung to the wood-panelled wall near the doorway. The clunk of the pendulum measured each step as Viola followed the Professor into the dimly lit room. He paused at a podium facing the centre of the room and scanned its panel with its array of buttons and levers. He flicked a switch and raised his head to face the shadows engulfing the room, looking much like her old university anatomy lecturer readying to give a lecture.

Gas flames rose and flickered, banishing the shadows to the far corners of the room. A pavilion of burgundy velvet hung from a chain in the centre of the ceiling. Hidden gears whirred above her head. Chains clinked and rattled as the cloth jerked upwards, revealing a wooden platform hidden beneath.

The cloth inched higher. Metal glinted tantalisingly at its edge. The cloth twitched, swooped upwards and swivelled to one side. With a clunk, the chain disengaged and retracted into the roof. The velvet cloth slumped and crumpled onto the floor.

Flickering flames reflected off a gigantic Armillary Sphere; the contraption had several layers of concentric brass rings; at its heart sat an elaborately carved, mahogany chair upholstered in rich velvet - black as the starless night sky, absorbing the surrounding light. Its arms flattened out into equally elaborately-carved control panels, each with etched bronze and silver dials and displays. Leather straps lay folded neatly on the seat.

"The Chronosphere." Professor Black grinned.

Viola's eye widened. "It certainly looks impressive," she said. Like something she'd expect to read about in the science fantasies Sir Archibald had mentioned. What did he call it again?

Professor Black rolled a portable step up to the platform and clicked it into place. He dusted off his hands and lifted a section of metal that circumscribed the contraption, opening an entry to the sphere.

"Is there a specific question you wish to answer?" asked Professor Black.

"Pardon?" Viola glanced back at him.

"Most travellers have something they need to know." A smile flickered across Professor Black's lips. "Perhaps you want to peek at your Christmas presents?"

Viola's fingers twitched. Tempting, but she needed to help Sir Archibald first.

Professor Black returned to the control panel and waited.

What would a woman like Miss Marchland want? Viola straightened her shoulders. "When will women get the vote in England?" she asked.

"I'm sorry, that's beyond the Chronosphere's reach."

"Then take me as far as your contraption allows, Professor."

"There is a limit of three days' excursion."

Viola's shoulders drooped. Only three days? How would she discover the truth in such a short time?

"It's a matter of energy. We need more power to extend the range of travel," said Professor Black. "For that we need more funds."

Don't we all? Viola cleared her throat, remembering the ruse: sister and research partner of a wealthy scientist. She lifted her chin and raised an over-exaggerated eyebrow. "Then you had better impress me with this demonstration," she said.

"Three days it is." Professor Black clapped his hands together.

"I will miss Christmas dinner?" And Polly's plum pudding.

The Professor shook his head. "No need." He cranked back the dial and pressed a button. "Christmas dinner it is, then?"

"How does it work?" Viola climbed the step and grinned. Two Christmases!

She gathered her skirt, tugged it close and negotiated the exposed end of the metal ring, clicking the metal bar back in place to re-join the circle. She wiggled her bustle into the chair's soft velvet. It was exceedingly comfortable, considering it didn't cater for womens' fashion.

Professor Black motioned toward the straps. Viola nodded, pulled the straps over her chest and lap, and buckled them snugly.

"Please place your hands on the armrests, Miss Marchland."

Viola lowered her hands onto the polished mahogany. Her heart fluttered. Was she really going to do this? She examined the panels: two circular dials were embedded in the left arm. A vertical cog-like dial jutted out of the panel near a numerical tumbler, on the left. If she just reached out her finger...

"Does this control the destination?" she asked.

Professor Black nodded. "I will control the machine from here." He turned another dial.

The numbers spun on the tumbler and settled: 25. 12. 1889.

Viola stretched out a finger. "Can *I* control it from here?" She noted the order of dials as he manipulated the controls.

"Best not. I can't guarantee your safety outside the set parameters, Miss Marchland. We can't predict the future, but we can learn from it."

Viola's finger snapped away from the controls. She surveyed the contraption. From the inside it resembled a brass cage, not unlike a Faraday cage... Or a spherical Ascension Chamber. She'd nothing but bad experiences in such chambers. Her fingers trembled. *What was she doing?* The straps constricted her movement. Her heart raced.

"Are you sure you wish to proceed?" Professor Black's hand hovered over the large toggle on the panel. He grinned, one corner curling up a bit too much for her liking.

Viola squirmed, feeling not unlike a fox trapped in a snare. Her gaze traced the skeletal rings surrounding her. Sir Archibald needed her help. She couldn't abandon him now. And how could she pass up such an opportunity?

She nodded. *For Sir Archibald, and for science.*

"Very well, but be careful not to stray too far. You must not change your future. Meddling in the time stream could be hazardous to one's very existence." He grasped the toggle. "You cannot go back to mend your mistakes."

"Why not?" Viola narrowed her eyelid; they were almost Sir Archibald's own words.

"We don't know the toll each trip takes on the physiology," he replied. "As a woman of science, you must understand my caution. Until there is enough empirical evidence to the contrary, I am reluctant to allow others to take such risks."

The grandfather clock's tick echoed throughout the room. Viola held her breath. The dials on the chair's arms whirred. Numbers spun at a dizzying pace on the barrel. A two, then a five. *December.* The final numbers clicked into place: *1889.*

Professor Black flipped the toggle in the middle of the panel. The rings shook, lifted and spun, whooshing slowly at first, then picking up pace in varying directions, forming a barrier between the outside world and Viola.

The clock's tick hastened.

Tick. Tick.

Tick, tick.

The hands spun.

Tick, tick, tick.

Tick, tick, tick.

The minute hand blurred, each rotation completed in less than a second. The hour hand followed in its wake.

The gas light faded. Sparks crackled from the sphere. Viola's breaths quickened. The room spun. She closed her eye and gripped the chair, willing her stomach back down her throat.

The cacophonous whine of the rings steadied, until it mimicked the tick of the clock. Locks of hair danced across Viola's face, caught in clicking zephyrs: cool, rhythmic, hypnotising. Her fingers relaxed. She cracked open her eyelid.

A hum filled the room as the thwack of the rings slowed. The breeze waned. The wall sconces flickered and roared to life.

Viola peered at the grandfather clock. Its minute-hand whirred.

Tick, tick, tick, tick.

Tick, tick,

Tick.

The minute hand nudged the twelve and clicked into place.

Gong.

Seven o'clock. The last brass ring spun past her vision, and slid into place.

Blood thrummed in her ears. The room spiralled around her, in decreasing waves, and eased to a halt. Viola blinked, struggling to steady her focus. This must have been how Sir Archibald felt after his trip last night. No wonder he was so befuddled.

The laboratory door opened. Professor Black stepped into the room. He straightened his cravat, tapped his pocket watch and slipped it into his waistcoat pocket.

"Merry Christmas, Miss Marchland. I do hope you like roast turkey."

Greenery filled the room, draping the paintings and lining the window. Bright red holly berries dotted the boughs. Miniature candles twinkled on the tips of the Christmas tree's branches. Hand-made cards dangled from string and skimmed the bottom of the mantelpiece. The fire crackled, its flames danced in the hearth, ebbing and flowing with the buzz of jolly conversation.

Professor Black had invited his sister, Phillipa Whitehead, and her husband to the dinner party. Mrs Whitehead had an air of an elegant woman forced to cope in trying circumstances: her impeccably-tailored midnight blue velvet gown glowed under the gaslight; green flashing eyes assessed her dinner companions and found herself in need of entertainment. Her crown of red curls bounced as she snatched up a Christmas cracker, thrust it in the direction of Mr Whitehead and giggled.

Mr Whitehead sighed and grabbed the paper.

"Now pull!" Mrs Whitehead jerked the cylindrical parcel toward her. Paper ripped and trinkets spilled onto the white tablecloth.

Viola peered through the silver-plated table candelabra and sipped more wine.

The feast was magnificent: roast turkey with cranberry sauce, steaming French potatoes, Brussels sprouts and honeyed peas. A dish of pork pies sat on one end of the table. The smell of cinnamon pervaded everything, though Viola could not place its source.

Mr Whitehead returned to chasing wayward peas around his plate. He sighed, flipped his fork and scooped a dollop of cranberry sauce onto a slice of turkey.

"Will you be attending the Royal Society's New Year's Eve Party, Miss Marchland?" asked Professor Black.

Viola shook her head and frowned. All this talk of parties! It was getting late and she was running out of time to find something to help Sir Archibald.

Professor Black's smile slipped. He placed his glass between strategically placed bowers of ivy. "I must apologise. Here we are talking of parties, when you, dear lady, are still in mourning."

Viola gulped down her mouthful of wine and lowered her gaze. Her black sleeves contrasted with the stark white of the tablecloth. She had forgotten her ruse. She must remember to play the part if she was to save Sir Archibald.

Phillipa Whitehead coughed mid-giggle. A Brussels sprout fell from her fork and plopped onto her plate.

"Oh, dear," Mrs Whitehead whispered. She silently placed her cutlery on the table.

Viola shifted in her seat. A change of subject was required.

"You are fortunate to find residence so close to King's College. But does the noise of the Chronosphere prove bothersome to the neighbours?"

"This was my father's house," replied Professor Black. "He owned it when the Royal Society of Science was still at King's. I acquired the buildings either side of the house some years ago before the houses nearby were vacated." Professor Black poured another glass of wine. "There are rumours of grand plans for expanding the College. Perhaps they will require more research assistants, Miss Marchland?"

"You're a scientist?" Mrs Whitehead scooped up the Brussels sprout. "I must admit I am lost when my brother tries to explain his latest..." She waved her hand in the air. "... Whatsit."

Mr Whitehead desisted from torturing his meal.

Viola pulled a handkerchief from her purse and eyed him as she dabbed her eye theatrically. "I was my brother's research assistant. The day of the accident..." She sniffed. "I was injured in the fulmination."

"Your tinted spectacles? Are they–?" Mrs Whitehead gasped.

"My eyes never fully recovered. I cannot abide any significant light source." Viola folded her handkerchief, placed it in her lap and nodded. "I am fated to live in the shadows and forever view the world through obsidian-coloured lenses."

All three guests stared at her with open mouths.

Viola bit her lip. Perhaps that was too much? She shifted in her chair. "I promised dear Albert I would honour his wishes to fund your chronological research."

Professor Black smiled. "I'm glad he deemed the Chronosphere worthy of consideration," he said.

Viola relaxed. They believed her.

"But I will require empirical evidence. Infallible proof." She twisted the corner of her handkerchief. "For the lawyers, you understand?"

Mr Whitehead glanced at Professor Black and sipped his wine.

"Of course," said Professor Black. "Something our earlier selves would not know?"

"That would suffice." Viola turned her wine glass and stared into the liquid. A patch of red light splashed across the cloth, bounced off the silver candelabra and flitted across the window. "Perhaps the big news of the day? Something that happened Christmas Eve? I require to finalise any endowment with the bank before I return to Europe tomorrow afternoon. I shan't be returning before Easter."

"Knowledge of the future is dangerous." Professor Black straightened the knife beside his plate.

Viola surveyed her dinner companions. She wouldn't find out anything here. She needed to get out of the house.

"However, I can say this," he said. "You first met my dear sister when you left, on your return to your original time."

"A boy ran out in front of my carriage," said Mrs Whitehead. "I still have the bruises!"

"I do hope he wasn't hurt?" asked Viola.

Professor Black placed his hand on his sister's elbow. "Only time will tell," he replied.

The butler's footsteps rang along the hallway. He wheeled a food trolley into the dining room and placed a platter of mince pies and a dish of Nesselrode pudding on the table, before retreating to the shadows.

"Nesselrode pudding," Mrs Whitehead clapped her hands. "My favourite."

Viola stared at the pudding. Her heart sank. The evening was almost finished; she was missing Christmas dinner with Henry and Sir Archibald will be... She swallowed. What was the point of a second Christmas if it wasn't spent with her friends?

Mrs Whitehead's hands fell onto the table. "You've gone pale, Miss Marshland. Are you unwell?"

Viola managed a faint smile. She mustn't forget the part she was playing - for Sir Archibald, and the Empire. She retrieved the handkerchief and sniffed. Watch yourself, Viola. Don't overdo it. *You'll give yourself away.* "Nesselrode pudding was Albert's favourite as well," she said.

Mrs Whitehead leaned closer and took Viola's hand. "There, there, my dear. A hot cup of tea will make you feel better."

Professor Black motioned to the butler. He emerged from the shadows, nodded and left the dining room.

Viola glanced at the clock. Almost midnight. Five hours and I've discovered nothing. Some detective she was! If she could contact Polly, find out if she has discovered anything over the past few days?

"Would it be safe to venture outside?" she asked. "I would dearly like to visit my friends. They will be so disappointed if they discovered I was still in London for Christmas, and didn't visit. I would only be an hour or two, and I promise not to mention the Chronosphere."

Mrs Whitehead folded her napkin and placed it on the table.

"That is the advantage of time travel, Miss Marshland." Professor Black leaned back in his chair. "When you return all will be as if this never happened. Time will continue on its original course. Only you shall remember this version, unless of course you decide to dine with us for Christmas again."

Viola's eye widened. "So time can be changed?" she asked. "But, if as you say, they won't remember any of this when I return to my original time, then what is the harm in visiting my friends?"

"The future is still unlived, Miss Marshland."

The butler returned and poured Viola a cup of tea. She picked up the tea cup and eyed Professor Black over the rim. Perhaps there was a way to gain more time, to find an answer to Sir Archibald's conundrum? She needed more time.

"And the past? Can it be relived?" she asked.

Professor Black straightened in his chair. Mrs Whitehead's cup rattled on its saucer.

"Can your machine travel back in time? I was wondering, no hoping, there was some possibility...?" She sniffed and caught her breath. Not too over-dramatic this time? "Perhaps I could return to the day of my brother's accident?"

"One can never go back," replied Professor Black

"Why not?" Viola lifted the cup to her lips and breathed in its warm vapour. It was sweet, with a hint of cinnamon and fruit.

"It's not safe." He waved away the tea pot and held up his wine glass. Mrs Whitehead followed suit.

"Travelling is too unpredictable." The butler filled his glass with wine. "Going forward we can glimpse what may, or may not, happen and there is less danger in corrupting one's future, as it has not yet arrived."

"But it has," said Viola.

"Has what?" asked Mrs Whitehead.

"The future is happening now," replied Viola.

Professor Black's tea cup remained untouched. Why was no one drinking their tea? She lowered her cup. She'd run afoul of a supposed innocent cup of tea before. She sniffed the vapour again. She could taste the sweetness.

"What if you triggered an accident that killed your mother?" asked Professor Black. He gulped the dregs of his wine. "Would you cease to exist?"

"If one changed the past, even in the smallest degree, who is to say what the consequences would be?" He picked up his tea cup and took a swig.

Viola held her breath and waited. Nothing happened.

"All this talk of time travel is making my head ache." Mrs Whitehead sighed.

Viola let her breath escape slowly. Her shoulders relaxed. *You're getting paranoid, Viola Stewart.* She raised her cup and took a sip. A fine mix of Darjeeling and Assam, with a hint of cinnamon and apple. "It tastes like apple cider."

"Clever, isn't it?" said Mrs Whitehead. "It's a special Christmas brew."

The clock chimed midnight.

"Time we get you back, Miss Marshland," said Professor Black.

Chapter 2: Propositions

The door to number twenty-three Stanhope Street clicked shut. Viola's ears still hummed from the aftereffects of returning to her original time. She pulled on her kid gloves and huffed. Nothing. She'd learned nothing. Her trip to the future had proved decidedly uninformative. But what had she expected? Answers never come that easy.

She glared back at the house. Sir Archibald was relying on her. His life depended on it, and she'd wasted her chance. She couldn't leave him to such an ignominious fate. Treason, indeed! Sir Archibald would never betray Queen nor country.

A chill breeze swirled around her, sending a shiver down her back. She pulled her visite tight and glanced across the street. A golden rim of fading sunlight edged the roofs of the vacant dwellings. Viola squinted to examine them. The lower windows were shuttered. Heavy curtains clothed those on the upper levels - a perfect vantage point to wait, and watch, until the household went to bed.

Only one trip? Ha! No matter the risk, she had to make another journey in that infernal machine. She'd studied the Professor. The procedure appeared simple enough: dial in the date, set the time. The Professor and his colleague had an engagement on New Year's Eve; that would provide a few hours to gather more information.

Professor Black's caution tugged at her memory: *You must not influence your future. You cannot go back to mend your mistakes.*

But what if she could? If there wasn't enough time while the Professor was at his party, she could continue her investigation on her return. Any other information, gleaned between now and New Year, could be delivered to her in the future. She *could* change Sir Archibald's fate.

Viola's head spun. Was it the contemplation of time travel, or the remnants of the return voyage? She took a deep breath. She'd have to tell Polly to deliver the information to her here on New Year's Eve.

How clever. Viola grinned. She would have two chances to investigate and can bring back the information with her - and prevent not only Sir Archibald's untimely demise but prove he is not a traitor.

Wheels clattered at the end of the street, reminding her of the noise of the Chronosphere. Viola paused on the steps. Her shoulders slumped. The machine would wake the house. They'd discover she'd used the machine and be waiting for her to return. How would she explain her intrusion?

Viola's mind raced; there had to be a solution. She just needed to apply some logic: Sir Archibald had said no one was home when he visited yesterday evening. They wouldn't be waiting for her, if she returned before she arrived. Perfect. She skipped down the steps.

The carriage rattled closer. Viola struggled to focus on the movement. Its black hulk blurred. The world lurched. Her stomach churned as she grabbed for the stone balustrade. Perhaps she'd not yet recovered from the effects of travelling?

A shadow flitted in the corner of her eye, moving toward the carriage. Viola blinked to clear her vision. A young boy darted across the street. Viola gripped the balustrade. "Watch out!"

The horse reared. The carriage shuddered.

The boy cursed as he skidded on the cobblestones and dashed into an alley.

"Steady. Steady." The driver jerked the reins tight. He twisted back toward the carriage. "Are you all right, Miss?"

"Are we there?" The voice was familiar.

The cab door opened. A woman in emerald velvet, her fiery hair almost hidden under an ornate hat, stepped out of the carriage and swirled up the steps. It was Professor Black's sister.

"I'm bruised head to toe." Mrs Whitehead glared at the driver. "Move along. You'll get nothing from me."

The driver's whip cracked above the horse's head. He grumbled and sped the cab off into the growing shadows.

"Are you all right, Mrs Whitehead?" asked Viola.

"Fine, thank you." Mrs Whitehead peered at Viola. "Have we met?"

Viola shook her head. Not yet. "I'm... Miss Marchland," she replied. "I believe your brother is expecting you."

Viola descended the steps and adjusted her tinted spectacles so she could spy Mrs Whitehead's reflection in the side mirror as she bustled through the front door.

Long shadows swathed the street. Small bursts of light erupted in the distance; the lamplighters were on their way.

Viola slipped into a narrow alley, between the buildings across the road, and made her way toward the servants' entrance. The back gate was unlatched. Viola slipped through the gate and eased the latch home.

The yard was pitch black, hidden in the shadow of the high fence, with no moon to cast useful light. Viola lifted the left tinted lens of her spectacles. It made little difference. If only she'd brought her night goggles. She felt her way along the wooden fence, and along the wall of the house until she found a door.

Viola lifted the silver locket from her neck, plucked out two of its amethyst-headed lock picks and searched out the keyhole. The door swung open. Not locked? Viola raised an eyebrow and entered.

The room was even darker than outside. Viola edged along the wall, her fingers feeling for any hint of where she was. She reached out into the darkness and groped the air.

Anything.

Her foot slammed into metal. A loud rattle skidded across the hard floor. She winced. A coal scuttle? If this was the kitchen, perhaps there's...

She shuffled forward, searching the room with her hands. Her nails scraped on wood. A bench? She wiped her hand along its surface. A cold metal object barred the way. She felt its shape. A lantern. Liquid sloshed. Viola smiled. She edged her hand along the edge, found a drawer and pulled it open. A faint smell of sulphur tugged at her nostrils. She struck a match. At last, some light.

The kitchen was small and bare. Flecks of rust peppered the dusty stove. A cracked jug sat on the bench. A coal scuttle lay by the opposite wall, near a discarded poker.

There was a muffled thump on the ceiling above. Viola held her breath, dimmed the lantern and cocked her ear toward the sound. Another faint knock, this time near the front of the house. Was someone upstairs?

She commandeered the poker and tiptoed toward the servants' steps. They were narrow, claustrophobic and in dire need of a good scrub.

The door at the top of the stairs opened out into a hallway. A faint light flickered through the front window at the far end, casting a glow onto the ceiling. The house was silent.

Viola stepped into the hall. The light faded. She crept along the hall toward the front room. The door was open and the curtains drawn. A horizontal shadow pierced the curtains. Viola tweaked the knob on the lantern.

The light reflected off a bronze telescope near the window. Its end peeked through a gap in the curtain. An armchair sat next to its supporting frame. A heavily-padded leather sofa faced the window, several feet away. An octagonal side table stood near the door.

Viola placed the lantern on the table and thrust out the poker in defence.

A faint aroma of fresh, spiced leather wafted in the air. A familiar, comforting smell. Viola closed her eye and drew a deep breath.

Henry? Her eye snapped open.

"Henry Collins, you should be convalescing. How dare you–?"

A warm hand clasped over her mouth.

Viola raised the poker. A firm grip stayed her hand.

"Do be quiet. The point of surveillance is not to let the subject know you are doing so." The voice was calm and concise, and one she'd heard before in the dark.

"That's impossible," she mumbled, as she turned her head slowly; bare skin brushed against her cheek. The poker twisted from her grip.

"Only improbable."

She glimpsed a well-tailored waistcoat, shirtsleeves rolled up to reveal athletic forearms. Metal glinted on her assailant's chest.

"Mr Wood?" The hand fell from her mouth. "You're a long way from Scotland," she said.

"Not 'Wood'." He ran his hand over his moustache.

"So, it is Mr Peabody?" Viola rubbed her wrist.

He dropped the poker near the empty fireplace and shook his head.

"Then what shall I call you?"

"Chester." He kissed her hand. "Mr Chester, at your service."

His hair smelled of new leather and spices. Viola's heart fluttered; her gaze followed him to the window.

"I must say you are looking... less bedraggled than last we met, Doctor Stewart." He sat on the armchair and realigned the telescope.

"Though black does not become you."

Viola peeked through the curtain; the telescope was trained at Professor Black's house.

"I hear congratulations are in order." Mr Chester straightened his waistcoat. "Though I hadn't thought his injuries were that serious."

Viola snatched her hand away from the curtain. "How did you know Doctor Collins was injured?" she asked.

Mr Chester peered through the telescope.

"You had me at a disadvantage in Scotland," he said. "I had been under the impression you were... unattached. Had I known, I would have behaved in a more appropriate manner."

Warmth spread up Viola's cheeks. Why hadn't she mentioned Henry? And why was she here, with a strange man? Unchaperoned. *At night!* Her fingers twitched. What would Lady Calthorpe think of her? Viola held her breath and stepped away from the window. She needed to concentrate.

"When is the happy day?" asked Mr Chester.

Viola retreated into the shadows. She just couldn't... How could she...? When Anne could be... She swallowed, not brave enough to say the word.

"We haven't set a date yet." Viola's thumb flicked at her engagement ring.

"I see." Mr Chester refocused the telescope and peered through the lens. "Have you ever considered a different vocation, Doctor Stewart? We need someone we can trust. The Department of Curiosities offers a life of independent adventure; no one following you, to keep an eye on you." He ran his fingers over his moustache.

"No one?" Viola edged back toward the window. Rivulets of rain smeared the glass.

"Of course, you would be bound by the Secrets Act. You could tell no one. Not even your fiancé."

Not tell Henry? Her heart thickened in her chest.

"But it would open avenues to pursue other investigations without hindrance," he continued.

Anne? Viola's eye widened. Could she finally discover her sister's fate? She moved another step closer. The smell of spiced leather tugged at her senses, clouding her thoughts, reminding her of Henry. Her shoulders relaxed. *She could be free to move on.*

Mr Chester turned away from the telescope. One corner of his lip curled.

Viola paused and crossed her arms. Had that been his intended design all along? To entice her into joining his precious Department? She peered through the window. Or was he trying to distract her from something else?

"Tell me, Mr Chester, if that is indeed your name," said Viola, "do you get lonely?"

Mr Chester remained silent.

"Is that why you attempt to entice me away from my fiancé, with the promise of liberty and emancipation?"

"Ah, the point of a secret department is for it to remain secret. No exceptions. A small price to pay for independence in a man's world, wouldn't you agree?"

Viola twisted the ring on her finger. She loved Henry. "But why should I, when I have both?"

Mr Chester cleared his throat and turned his attention back to the telescope. Viola smiled and eyed the sofa behind them. A greatcoat lay crumpled on one end.

"I assume you are in London on a Department matter, Mr Chester?" she asked. It was time for him to share *his* secrets. Viola moved the coat aside, sat on the sofa and rearranged her skirts. She could play these games as well as he. "Or are you following me?" she asked.

Mr Chester shook his head. His chair squeaked on the floorboards as he rose.

"Just a pleasant coincidence." He sat down on the couch beside Viola. His dark hair fell over one eye.

Viola straightened the ring on her finger and smiled. She was onto his tricks. She'd not be distracted again. "May I enquire as to your interest in Professor Black?"

Mr Chester remained silent.

"Or shall I be required to sign more papers before you can answer that?"

"No need," he replied. "Remember our adventure in Scotland?"

"The smugglers?" She still had an adorable mechanical Bot as a souvenir. Viola bit her cheek, trying not to smile.

He nodded.

"I followed their trail here. Professor Black's storehouse is stocked with ill-gotten gains." He leaned back in his chair. "Your turn, Doctor Stewart. What brings you to Stanhope Street?"

"I'm..." It was now his turn to remain uninformed; she would not make it easy for him. "Helping a friend."

"Yes." He glanced in Viola's direction. "Tell me more about Sir Archibald Huntington-Smythe."

Viola caught her breath. "How did you–?"

"Come now, Doctor Stewart. I've read your dossier, remember. Friend or not, he has been associating with individuals of dubious standing."

Viola jumped to her feet. *Never!*

"Sir Archibald's reputation is beyond reproach. He would never..." She crossed over to the telescope and stared out of the window. Only one light remained burning in Professor Black's house.

"But is he trustworthy?" asked Mr Chester.

"I trust him with my life," she replied.

"Nevertheless, I need to know how he is involved, Doctor Stewart.

There are plans in motion. And I have been sent to prevent them."

Ah, there it was. Viola spun on her heel. "So, all this has been to gain my trust, so you can extract information on Sir Archibald?"

"He has a privileged position as personal physician to the Queen. If he was to use that position, or was coerced into doing so..." Mr Chester pinched his lip between steepled fingers. "There would be serious ramifications, not just for your friend, but for the Empire." He stared at her over the top of his hands. "So, I ask you again, Doctor Stewart, tell me how Sir Archibald is involved in all this."

"Professor Black is petitioning for funds to expand his research."

"No blackmail?" he asked.

Viola's heart sank into her stomach. Was Professor Black planning to blackmail Sir Archibald? "It's not what you think," she replied.

"No?"

"No." Viola clenched her fists. She spoke quickly: "Sir Archibald has implored me to find the truth. He would *never* give in to blackmail."

"You are a loyal friend, Doctor Stewart, but I–"

"No, listen." She strode toward him. "Sir Archibald dies tomorrow."

Mr Chester's hands fell onto his lap.

"They have a time machine. I think they plan to–"

Mr Chester stood slowly.

"They have what?" The colour drained from his face.

Viola raised an eyebrow. She'd never seen him rattled before.

"Then it is true?" His voice cracked. He moved toward the window, each step slow and deliberate, and sat in the chair next to the telescope.

"Yes, I've seen it," she replied.

"And it works?" He pressed his eye against the telescope's eyepiece.

"It appears so." Viola straightened her shoulders. "I had Christmas dinner with Professor Black and his sister in two days' time."

Mr Chester sat in silence, staring at the house for several seconds; there was no witty retort, no flashing smile. He sniffed, unhooked the telescope and collapsed the tube with a snap, and turned to face Viola.

"The Department thanks you for your co-operation, Doctor Stewart. I commend your loyalty to Sir Archibald." His moustache twitched. "And to your fiancé." He placed the telescope in a velvet-lined box. "But I have a duty to a higher authority. Sir Archibald must be detained for further questioning and the machine will be confiscated."

"No! I need that machine. I need to prove his innocence." Viola grabbed Mr Chester's arm. "Just give me one more day."

He flipped the latch on the box closed. "Very well. I will allow Sir Archibald one more day. But if you warn him, you will be committing treason." The gleam returned to his eyes. "And your fiancé will not be pleased."

Viola released the grip on his arm. "I can make my own decisions, Mr Chester. I don't need anyone's approval. Not Henry's, and certainly not yours."

"I can see why Doctor Collins admires you." He bowed his head. "I will escort you home." He retrieved his greatcoat, placed it on Viola's shoulders and gestured in the direction of the door. "But you are not to enter Professor Black's house. That machine is now under Department jurisdiction."

"But, you just said–"

"I must insist, Doctor Stewart. You don't realise the danger you have courted. Professor Black has dangerous allies."

"Then how shall I prove Sir Archibald's innocence?"

"I will complete the investigation," replied Mr Chester.

"Do I have a choice?"

"No. You must trust me, Doctor Stewart."

Rain tapped on the window, obscuring the street. Viola slipped her arms into the sleeves of Mr Chester's coat and pulled it tight.

"You must earn it, Mr Chester."

Flames licked the fireplace. A blackened chunk of wood shifted, fell to the floor of the hearth and crumbled into charred fragments. A shiver flitted down Archibald's neck. He puffed on his pipe; his gaze tracked its smoke as it swirled toward the fireplace and mingled with the flames.

Viola had been gone too long. He should have handled this himself.

The parlour door swung open. Polly entered, settled a food tray on the side table, and started to light the gas wall sconces. A warm glow filled the room.

He glanced at the clock on the mantelpiece. Almost eight o'clock.

"Any news?" he asked.

Polly poked the fire. "Sir, I'm worried," she whispered.

Archibald shook his head and returned his attention to the dying fire. Henry would never forgive him if anything had happened to Viola.

Hooves clopped on the cobblestones outside. A carriage rattled to a stop. Archibald twisted in his chair. Rain pounded on the darkened windows.

"At last." He sucked on his pipe. Smoke filled his lungs; his body relaxed.

There was a tap on the front door. Polly smiled and skipped from the room. Footsteps echoed in the hall.

Polly hurried through the door, twisting the corner of her apron.

"It's about time." Archibald jumped to his feet and spun to face the doorway.

"Doctor Collins to see Miss Viola." She took Henry's coat, stepped aside and shook off the droplets of rain.

Henry leaned heavily on an ornate walking stick. A mechanical splint supported his left leg. His face was pale, his waistcoat crooked, his jacket dishevelled. He hobbled toward the fireplace and collapsed into the chair facing Archibald.

Archibald lowered himself back into his chair and tucked his pipe under the edge of the supper tray.

"You should be resting," said Archibald. "You could end up with a permanent limp. Or worse..." He glared at Henry through narrowed eyelids. "You could require my more advanced mechanical services."

Curls of pipe smoke escaped from under the tray. Henry raised his eyes and looked Archibald in the eye. "You said you'd give up that vile habit," said Henry.

Archibald waved away stray wisps of smoke and straightened his spectacles. Polly hovered near the doorway, avoiding Henry's gaze.

"Viola missed tea this afternoon," said Henry.

Archibald and Polly exchanged glances.

"Come on, Archie. I may have injured my leg, but my mental faculties are intact. What has Viola gotten herself into?"

Archibald's fingers twitched toward his pipe. Henry's moustache twitched. "Where is your Mistress?" he asked Polly.

Polly straightened her apron and bit her lip.

"It's not the girl's fault, Henry."

"Tell me what is going on, Archie!" Henry gripped his cane and stomped it on the floor.

Archibald took a deep breath and steadied his hands. "Viola makes her own decisions," he said.

Henry leaned closer. "If anything has happened to her..." His moustache drooped.

"Viola is an intelligent woman and quite capable of looking after herself."

Henry slumped back into his chair. "But does the world know that?"

Rivulets of water rolled down Viola's neck. She flipped up the collar of her borrowed coat and dashed to her front door, turning only briefly to watch the carriage trundle off around the corner into High Street.

Light flooded out of the open door and spilled onto the porch. She dashed up the steps.

Polly stood in the doorway and curtsied. "Doctor Collins is here to see you, Miss."

Viola glanced into the hall. Sir Archibald hovered behind Polly, fidgeting with his spectacles. Henry hobbled from the parlour to join him, one leg encased in a jumble of whirring gears and pistons attached to a metal leg brace.

"Hello, Vi." He shifted his weight onto his walking cane and frowned.

"Henry Collins! You should be–"

"You're wet," replied Henry.

Polly closed the door behind Viola and stared at the floor.

Water dripped from lank curls of hair and seeped under Viola's bodice. Drops ran off the cuffs of the greatcoat and collected on her fingertips. She flicked them to the ground. Drenched skirts clung to her calves. She shivered and glanced at her feet and the ever-expanding puddle of water that collected there.

Polly took the greatcoat and examined it as she hung it on the hallstand. Henry's gaze followed the coat.

"New coat?" asked Henry. His mechanical brace clicked as he shifted his weight. "Sir Archibald was just about to tell me about his afternoon."

Polly glanced at Viola, then at Henry and cleared her throat. "I'll fetch some towels."

Henry waited until Polly had left the hall and turned to Sir Archibald. "Weren't you, Archie?"

"The jig is up, I'm afraid, old girl." Sir Archibald sighed and shoved his hands into his jacket pockets.

Viola stepped forward; one foot sploshed in the water.

"It's a matter of life and death," said Viola. "You are injured. We had no choice. Sir Archibald dies tomorrow. Professor Black wouldn't allow him to travel a second time."

"Travel where?" asked Henry.

"When," whispered Sir Archibald.

"What?" Henry raised an eyebrow. "Did you say: *Archie dies?* How could you possibly know that?"

"I travelled through time, Henry!" Viola grinned.

"You what? Time travel isn't possible." Henry turned to face Sir Archibald. "What is going on, Archie?"

"Sir Archibald will die tomorrow, and I travelled forward in time to find out how to prevent it." Viola wiped her hand on her bodice and placed it on Henry's.

Henry shook his head.

"Show him, Sir Archibald," said Viola.

Sir Archibald retrieved the crumpled newspaper from his jacket pocked, flicked it open and handed it to Henry.

Henry read the headline, dropped the newspaper on the hall table and leaned on his cane.

"Is this true? That scientist at the Meeting? He was serious?"

Sir Archibald nodded. "We've both travelled, Henry."

"I had Christmas dinner with the Professor," said Viola. "It's all true. We can't let Sir Archibald die. I have to return. To save him."

"And Sir Archibald thought it prudent for you to go alone?" asked Henry. "I won't have it, Vi. It's too dangerous."

"You won't–?" Viola's heart froze. She released Henry's hand. "You don't own me, Henry Collins. You don't get to tell me what I can or can't do. Not now." Her thumb clicked on her engagement ring. "Not ever."

Viola's foot slapped in the puddle. Drips quivered off the hem of her skirt and plopped onto her boots, seeping under the laces.

Polly scurried in with a bundle of towels in her arms. She presented one to Viola and bent down to mop up the floor.

Viola examined the towels as Polly soaked up the water. She ran her toe through the puddle beneath her and eyed Mr Chester's coat on the hall stand. It hung, in a heavy, sopping mass, next to Sir Archibald's dry coat. Bone dry. How had he managed to keep dry? *It will be raining on Christmas day.*

"Sir Archibald, you had Christmas dinner with Professor Black?" she asked.

"Roast beef and Brussels sprouts." He licked his lips.

"Did it rain when you found the paperboy outside, in the street?"

"No, it was a glorious night. Not a cloud in the sky."

No rain? Perhaps the future had been altered? Had Sir Archibald's interaction with the paperboy generated a new temporal crossover and broken down the logic of causality? The Professor had warned her of the possibility. But how? She had heeded their warnings and not left the house. She leaned on the hall table. And how could that possibly affect the weather?

"It rained when I had Christmas dinner," she whispered. "No, something isn't right."

"Viola?" Henry stepped forward. Deep lines etched his forehead. "Polly, fetch your Mistress a warm blanket."

Viola's eye widened; she stepped back.

"It wasn't raining." She shoved the towel into Henry's hands. "Don't you see? I have to go back." She wrenched open the hall table drawer and snatched up her gilded pistol and night goggles.

"But–?" His moustache drooped.

Viola stared into Henry's bright blue eyes. Fine wrinkles had formed at the corners.

"Trust me, Henry." She grabbed a coat and dashed out into the street in search of a Brougham cab.

Chapter 3:
A Chronic Disaster

Viola held her breath and felt for the floor in the dark with her toe. It touched solid ground. She let out her breath and pulled her skirts free of the windowsill, her boot snagging in a snarl of silk. She lost her balance, tumbled into the room and rolled headfirst into a piece of unseen furniture, with a thud. A faint rip made her wince.

Distant lamp light outlined an opening on the other side of the room. Voices wafted through the doorway.

"But you promised!" It was Professor Black. His voice was muffled.

Viola ducked behind the unidentified furniture.

"You said if I delivered the surgeon–," he hissed.

"You have not completed your side of the bargain." A woman's voice. Viola strained to hear.

The light receded. Viola waited, until the only noise she could hear was her own breathing. She flipped up the ruching of her bustle skirt, and reached into the pocket concealed under her bustle to retrieve her night goggles and slipped them on over her eye patch. Large, dark shapes filled the room. She clicked an auxiliary lens into position. Shadowy outlines of chairs and sofas resolved out of the dark. This must be the parlour.

Viola picked her way through the room toward the hall. Professor Black and his conspirator were nowhere to be seen. She hugged the wall and made her way along the hall until she found a door. She tested the knob. The door clicked open.

The room was dark. She placed her ear against the crack and listened. All was silent. She took a deep breath, slipped inside and scanned the room. Large square shapes lined the walls. A low, rectangular outline suggested a desk on the far side. Behind it was a smaller, paler square area on the wall.

Viola inched her way forward, feeling her way. She glanced over the desk: a blotter, pen and ink, a pile of letters, textbooks. A pile of notes sat on one end, next to an etched metal casket. She moved the desk chair out of the way, careful not to make a noise.

A portrait of a serene blonde woman beckoned Viola closer. She turned her attention to the intriguing area hidden on the wall behind it, unhooked the portrait and propped it against the desk. A fine crack outlined a two-foot square area of one of the wooden panels. She tapped on the wall. It sounded hollow. A hidden cupboard? A safe?

Viola clicked another lens in front of her goggles and ran her fingers over the panel. A slight recess marked the keyhole. She extracted two amethyst-headed lock picks from the silver locket around her neck. There was a satisfying click. She slipped the lock picks home.

Gears whirred in the wall. The wall panel slid open to reveal a wall safe. Viola peeked into the void. What could be so important?

Inside was a mahogany box, approximately one foot square, assorted loose papers and several document pouches. Viola caught her breath. This could be what she was looking for! Perhaps risking another journey to the future wasn't necessary after all?

She eased the box out of the safe and placed it on the desk, then retrieved a pouch and unwound the cord securing it shut. She flipped through the contents. It was a dossier.

Viola's heart raced. She grabbed the remaining document pouches, five in all. She opened another pouch, and another. The fourth was a

dossier on Professor Marchland. Large capital letters were printed across the front page in a steady, confident hand:

EXTINGUISHED: FILE CLOSED/COMPLETE

Dead? Was Professor Black behind Professor Marchland's death? She closed the pouch. Was there a dossier on Sir Archibald? Viola swallowed and picked up the final folder. Her fingers trembled as she unwound the cord, slipped out the pages and read the handwritten notation on the front page:

IN PROGRESS.

She turned the page:

SIR ARCHIBALD HUNTINGTON-SMYTHE

Her heart sank. Poor Archie. She skimmed the pages, straining to read the notes, even with the augmented vision of her goggles. There were pages of personal information, a listing of his daily routine and detailed information of his access to the Queen. There was even a list of his favourite foods.

One page had a report on Professor Black's lecture at the Research Meeting. Another detailed his plot to gain Sir Archibald's confidence and a plan to persuade him to travel forward to Christmas day. There was even mention of Sir Archibald's procurement of the newspaper. Viola gasped. The Professor knew he had it!

In the margin was a scribbled notation:

This is an opportune moment to act, as subject's friend, Police Surgeon Doctor Henry Collins, is unable to assist due to a recent injury. This will reduce possible support or assistance during the operation and increase subject's isolation.

Viola shoved the pages back into the pouch and wrapped the cord around it. She snatched up Professor Marchland's dossier and paused. She eyed the box. What else could the Professor be hiding? She flipped the brass latch and eased open the lid.

A lifeless wax mask stared back at her. Viola's eyes widened. It was Sir Archibald! She'd seen similar craftsmanship before: a wax mask of Arthur Doyle made by an ex-employee of Madame Tussaud's - part of a foiled plot by the Men in Grey. Viola slumped into the chair. Was Professor Black involved in one of their plots? What had Sir Archibald stumbled into?

Voices drifted down the hall into the room. She slapped the lid shut and tucked the box under her arm. The voices grew louder.

"You got rid of him." Professor Black was returning.

Viola shoved the remaining pouches back into the wall safe.

"No matter, Marchland brought us Sir Archibald - before he had a change of heart, before he couldn't stomach the idea of betrayal." This time the woman's voice was clear.

Viola's heart jumped into her throat. It was Mrs Whitehead. She hadn't seemed the leader type.

"But you removed him before he could give us the money," whined the Professor. "I can't finish my research without it."

"You'll get your money from his estate. The sister doesn't suspect a thing. Just make sure she doesn't find you when it's all done."

"I can't wait that long. You must pay me what you promised now."

The footsteps paused. They were close. Viola's heart thumped as she strained to hear.

"You haven't completed your end of the bargain," said Mrs Whitehead. "I need the surgeon's agreement. You will not get your payment until he provides us with the information we need when he returns. This time make sure you give him enough of that drug."

"Will the mask be convincing?"

"Just keep him out of the way until the task is complete. He must take the blame. I'll be leaving as soon as this farce is over."

Viola's heart froze. So they are behind the assassination attempt and intend to blame it all on Sir Archibald. She tugged on the safe door. Cogs whirred; the lock clicked. The footsteps quickened.

Viola glanced at the wall portrait leaning against the desk and frowned. There was no time to replace it. She snatched up the two pouches and ducked under the desk.

The door creaked. The desk's shadow flowed up the wall as their lamp moved closer. Gas hissed. Viola tucked herself further under the desk to avoid the light. Footsteps crossed the room. Closer. Closer. Viola held her breath.

"But what if he doesn't return tomorrow?" asked Professor Black, his voice clear.

"Make sure he does, and that he does not leave here. That is what you are being paid for. My job is to ensure the Fat Empress is eliminated. We must have control over–"

The footsteps stopped.

"Check the files," hissed Mrs Whitehead.

Footsteps hurried to the wall. The door whirred open.

Viola reached into her pocket for her pistol. She had two shots. At this close range, it should be enough. Her fingers trembled. She'd rather not–

He gasped. "The box is *gone*."

"We need that box!" Mrs Whitehead's boots clicked across the room.

Viola peeked out from under the desk. Professor Black was only a few feet away. He turned to face Mrs Whitehead, his face twisted in fear.

"It's not my– " He paused, directing his attention toward the desk. He took a step closer.

Viola let out a slow, controlled breath.

His grip on her arm was stronger than she expected. He yanked her clear of the desk. Viola's boots scraped on the floor as she struggled to break free. Her pistol jerked out of her hand and skittered along the wooden floor.

Professor Black dragged her onto the chair.

The box clattered onto the floor. Viola clutched the pouches; she couldn't lose proof of Sir Archibald's innocence. She bowed her head, her hair falling over her face, and stared at the box. She needed its contents to prove their plan.

Professor Black picked up the box.

"Ah, Miss Marchland. What an unpleasant surprise this is." Mrs Whitehead clasped Viola's chin in her hand, lifted up her face and slipped her goggles onto her forehead. She glared at Viola's eye patch. "Not Miss Marchland?"

"The one-eyed doctor!" Professor Black drew in a sharp breath. The box thudded on the desk. "She's a known associate of Sir Archibald, works with Collins in the Police morgue."

Mrs Whitehead sneered. "You were supposed to ensure all of Huntington-Smythe's associates were accounted for."

"She was considered of no consequence," said the Professor. "After all, what can a woman do?"

"You little– " Viola lunged forward.

Mrs Whitehead pushed her back into the chair, glared at Professor Black and raised her hand to him.

"Am I of no consequence?" she hissed.

Professor Black flinched and darted to the opposite side of the desk.

"What can we do?" he mumbled.

"We do nothing."

A crack of splintering wood echoed down the hallway.

Mrs Whitehead lowered her hand. "You deal with her. There will be no loose ends. I trust you can perform that simple task?" She picked up the box, turned on her heel and strode out of the room. The door clicked shut behind her.

Professor Black circled around the desk and positioned himself between Viola and the door.

"How could you sell your soul to the likes of The Society?" asked Viola.

Professor Black avoided her gaze. "You don't say no to The Society."

Viola shook her head. "I'd never sell my soul to the Men in Grey. Never."

"You don't understand. I had no choice. The Royal Society refused to fund my experiments. They laughed at me. I needed the money to prove them wrong." He took a deep breath and opened the metal casket on the desk. "You must understand; you're a scientist." Glass rattled. He removed a vial of clear liquid and examined the label.

"It's used to sedate the target when a mask is made." He flicked off the stopper and plunged the syringe into the vial.

Viola scanned the floor for the pistol. A hint of gold glinted under the edge of the desk. She slowly stretched out her leg. Almost there. She pointed her toe and tapped the pistol closer.

Professor Black glanced at the syringe and frowned. "Of course, I'm not a physician." He drew more liquid into the syringe, and smiled at Viola. "I'm told it's like falling asleep."

Viola's breath quickened. She had an aversion to needles. She held her breath and lunged for the pistol.

The vial smashed on the desk. Professor Black charged forward with the syringe. Viola snatched up the pistol. She could not allow Mrs Whitehead to use the Chronosphere. Viola shot wildly in the Professor's direction. The syringe skittered along the floor in the opposite direction to the flailing Professor. She jumped to her feet, clutching the pouches tightly, dashed toward the door and slammed it shut behind her.

Tall brick walls lined the alley beside Professor Black's residence. Archibald rattled the gate blocking the way to the back yard. It was locked.

"Hurry up, Archie." Henry's leg brace clicked as he paced behind him. "Put your back into it, man."

Archibald retreated a couple of yards along the alley and charged the gate. A soft crack of wood broke the silence. A pain shot through his shoulder.

"Excellent," said Henry.

Archibald grimaced, clutched his arm and flexed his fingers. Nothing was broken. He peered at Henry, a vague shadow in the darkness. Archibald struggled to focus. Was that another shadow behind Henry? A distorted hump-backed figure loomed closer, raising a bar in the air.

"Henry, move."

The figure trotted closer. Archibald pushed Henry to one side; gears whined. The figure rushed at the gate. A thud, then a crack. It retreated a few steps.

"Don't just stand there," it scolded. "We've got to get in there; she'll need assistance."

"How do you know–?" Henry straightened his back.

"On three?" asked the stranger.

Archibald's shoulder throbbed. Pain shot along his arm. He flexed his fingers. He couldn't break through on his own. He had to help Viola. He joined the newcomer, glad of the assistance, and nodded. "One. Two..."

"Three." They dashed toward the gate in unison.

The gate splintered at the latch. Archibald tumbled into the yard, struggling to keep his balance. Henry's whirring footsteps followed them.

Archibald dusted shards of wood from his coat and peered into the darkness. "We should have brought some light," he said.

There was a clunk and hiss. A ghostly blue light erupted around them.

"Glad to be of assistance," said their new companion.

Archibald examined the illuminated figure beside him, a box-like pack harnessed to his back. A glass cylinder crackled with buzzing light, in his hand, revealing a green waistcoat. A badge glimmered on his chest: a lightning bolt set upon a brass cog. He flipped his dark hair out of his eyes and grinned.

"Excellent," said Archibald. "Shall we continue?"

"And you are?" asked Henry.

"Mr Chester." He shook Archibald's hand. "And you are Sir Archibald Huntington-Smythe?" He turned to face Henry. "You must be the fiancé? Doctor Collins, isn't it?"

"Pardon?" Henry's moustache twitched.

Mr Chester turned his light tube upward and skimmed the light across the sky and toward the wall. "Doctor Stewart has told me all about you," he said.

"I don't recall her mentioning you." Henry straightened and glared at Chester.

"She wasn't at liberty to." Chester seemed oblivious to Henry's displeasure. He surveyed the end of the yard, shone his light tube at the back corner of the house and moved closer to the wall.

"Why not?" Henry stood his ground.

Chester paused and sighed. "Have you not heard of the Secrets Act?" he asked.

"Of course. I've bloody well signed it!" Henry strode after him; the leg brace cogs whined and clicked in protest.

"Ah, yes. I'd forgotten," said Chester. "It seems we have been working on the same investigation."

Archibald eyed Chester. He worked for the Empire? What did he know? Surely Viola wouldn't have confided in him?

Henry stopped beside Chester and thrummed his fingers on the head of his cane. "How do you know Doctor Stewart?" he asked, not taking his eyes off him.

"She assisted me in an investigation, in Scotland." Chester lifted a section of wood from the wall and shone the light into a cavity.

Archibald pushed his spectacles up his nose and regarded the two men: dark hair and moustaches, tailored waistcoats, determined posture. Two identical bucks intent on winning. But they were wasting time.

He took a deep breath. Viola was alone. In danger. And it was because of him. His footsteps rang through the yard as he marched ahead of them, toward the house into the darkness. His foot rammed into something solid; he tripped, slamming his hand down onto a concrete edge. He felt his way along the obstacle and onto the ground beneath his feet. Cobblestones? In the back yard?

He stood slowly and dusted off his palms. "I say, Henry, I've found something."

The light tube bobbed closer. It created a puddle of pale blue light at his feet, revealing cobblestoned paving and footpath.

"A street in the back yard?" asked Henry.

Archibald was already at the house, climbing the stairs to the door. "Be quick, man. We've wasted too much time."

Chester and Henry followed, dodged an unlit lamp post and joined him. The eerie blue light glowed on the knocker: a perfectly aligned brass lion's head. Faded paint flaked around it.

"A duplicate door?" Archibald ran a gloved finger along the edge of the door.

"And there's a hidden control box, with a pulley mechanism and pipes, in the wall," said Chester. "I think I've managed to turn off the gas. Darkness should slow the Professor down." He pointed to the heavens. "There's also a system of water pipes and light conduits leading up and over the yard."

Archibald's hand went to his jacket pocket. The newspaper? "An elaborate set up to replicate the front of the house?" he whispered.

"For what purpose?" asked Henry.

Archibald and Chester looked at each other. *Chester knew.* Archibald swallowed. But how? Viola would never betray him to a stranger.

A shot rang from inside the house.

"Viola!" Henry rushed forward and rattled the door handle. It was locked. He slammed his shoulder into the door. The knocker jiggled.

Chester shoved his crowbar into the doorjamb, just above the lock. All three men grabbed the bar and pushed. The door opened with a thunderous crack.

Henry pushed past them into the hallway. Archibald followed behind him. They stood in a hallway identical to that at the front of the house.

"Which way did the shot come from?" asked Henry.

The door slammed behind them.

Viola's footsteps padded on the carpet runner as she hurried along the hallway. This part of the house was unfamiliar. She had to find her way back to the front hall, to get her bearings so she could find the laboratory. Mrs Whitehead could not be allowed to use the Chronosphere.

She heard muffled voices ahead in the darkness. Perhaps she'd caught up with her. Viola turned the corner and froze. Four pale figures stood out from the background. She stepped back, adjusted her night goggles and peered around the corner.

A tall figure walked ahead of the group, carrying a gas lamp. Another covered the rear, brandishing a short pole with a curved end. One of the herded men walked with a limp.

"Keep moving." The rear-guard prodded the two men in front of him.

Viola crept closer, careful to stay out of the lamp light. Gears whirred faintly from the direction of the limping man. Henry? She clenched the pistol. She had one shot left. Her finger twitched. What if she missed? She'd proved a poor marksman in the past. She waited until the rear-guard separated from the group. She held her breath and pulled the trigger.

The leader halted, turned on his heel and grabbed Henry. A red stain spread on his comrade's trousers. Viola recognised Sir Archibald in the lamp light; she'd seen the two guards before - the Professor's butler and his footman. The butler thrust the lamp forward and yelled. The footman clutched his knee and crumpled to the ground and screamed, his face contorted in agony.

Viola gasped. She'd never shot anyone before - well, not successfully. Her hand trembled as she raised her pistol. Perhaps the butler wouldn't notice there were no bullets left. He flinched; Henry twisted free from his grip.

Sir Archibald grabbed Henry's cane and slammed it home into the butler's stomach and, with a practised swing, curved it around and brought it crashing down on the scoundrel's skull.

Henry teetered back against the wall, his leg brace clicking uncontrollably.

Sir Archibald raised the cane in the direction of the injured footman. He raised his hand and shook his head. Sir Archibald snatched up the dropped lamp and handed it, and the cane, to Henry, one eye still trained on the fallen footman. He grabbed the footman's arm and rolled him onto his side, undid his own cravat and wrapped it around the footman's wrists.

Viola lunged toward Henry, dodging the fallen men. She ran her hand over his arms. "Are you injured?" she whispered to Henry.

Henry shook his head and pushed himself away from the wall. She dropped her hands and stepped back. "Henry, you promised..."

"But I–"

"I insisted we come." Sir Archibald stepped forward.

Viola raised an eyebrow. She didn't have time to discuss the issue; she had to make sure Mrs Whitehead didn't reach the laboratory first.

"We'll talk later." She glanced along the hall in the direction from which they'd come. "Where does it lead?" she asked.

"To the back of the house," replied Henry.

Viola's shoulders slumped. Not the direction she'd hoped; she needed to find the front hall. She pressed the mahogany box and file pouches into Sir Archibald's hands. "Here's the proof we were looking for."

"Viola..." Henry clasped her hand. "It's not safe."

"You're in no state for heroics," she kissed his hand, "and Sir Archibald needs to guard these ruffians." She slipped the night goggles over her eye patch. "Trust me, Henry," she whispered.

Henry released her hand and gave her his cane. "Be careful."

Viola smiled and turned to Sir Archibald. "Look after Henry."

Sir Archibald nodded.

"I have an assassination to stop." She gathered up her skirts and spun on her heel to face the opposite direction. "I have to find Mrs Whitehead before she uses the Chronosphere."

"But it's... " Sir Archibald's voice faded as Viola ran down the hall in search of the Professor's laboratory.

Viola watched the figure from behind a curiosity cabinet. A large carpet bag snagged on the ruffles of the figure's folded skirts. It had to be Mrs Whitehead; she would lead her to the laboratory. Until then, Viola watched and waited. She followed her quarry past the servants' stairs and into a wide hallway. Viola glanced along the hall. An Oriental vase sat on a hall table near the door at the far end. It was the front hall. Viola counted the doors and smiled. Mrs Whitehead had led her to the laboratory.

Viola hefted the cane in her hand. She could not allow Mrs Whitehead to access the Chronosphere. The Queen's life was in danger and Sir Archibald's reputation threatened. She had to stop Mrs Whitehead from entering the laboratory.

Viola held her breath, crept closer and raised the cane. Mrs Whitehead paused and turned. Viola squeezed her eye shut and swung the cane. For the Empire!

There was a crashing thud. She opened her eye. Pieces of shattered vase lay strewn amongst the crumpled skirts of the unconscious woman at her feet. The carpet bag lay on the floor, its contents scattered across the floor.

Viola gasped. Her fingers trembled as she removed her glove and held her hand under Mrs Whitehead's nostrils. A faint breath warmed her fingers. Viola sighed. Thank God, she was alive. Viola gathered up the document pouches and slipped them into the bag. Perhaps these would help save other unfortunates from the clutches of The Society? She snatched up the bag and rushed into the laboratory.

The laboratory was dark. Viola reached up to the nearest wall sconce and pulled the chain. The pipes remained silent. Viola frowned. The gas was off. Would there be any power to the Chronosphere?

She examined the room. The velvet pavilion covered the machine in the centre of the room. The control pedestal stood a few feet away. The tick of the antique grandfather clock near the doorway behind her echoed through the laboratory.

Viola placed the carpet bag next to the control pedestal. She glanced over the levers and dials on the panel. She'd assisted on enough of Sir Archibald's contraptions to know how to create a critical pressure surge.

Her heart raced. Could she do it? Could she destroy another scientist's life work? She flexed her fingers. The Men in Grey had many agents; if she didn't, there would be someone else to take Mrs Whitehead's place.

She flicked a switch on the left of the panel. The velvet cloth jerked. Gears whirred. Chains ratcheted the cloth upward. Viola wiped her clammy hands on her skirt, cranked a dial on the right of the panel and pressed the button next to the dial. Her breaths quickened.

The Chronosphere hummed into life.

Viola closed her eye and concentrated on each breath, filling her lungs as deep as her stays would allow.

One.

Slow.

Two.

Deliberate.

Three.

Her pulse slowed. She opened her eye. Her fingers relaxed and dropped onto the next switch in the sequence.

A crackling buzz filled the room. Viola's night goggles flooded with light. She squinted in pain and flicked them onto her forehead. The room shone with an eerie blue glow, reflecting off the Chronosphere's rings, casting bright lines onto the walls like an enchanted cage.

"Stand aside, Doctor Stewart!"

Viola turned slowly. Mr Chester stared at the Chronosphere, as if enthralled. He held a light tube, a compact, more sophisticated version of the one she'd seen in the storage cellar at Marylebone Police Station. Blue lightning sparked from one end, filling the tube with light.

"This machine is now the property of the Department of Curiosities," he said.

"But I must stop the assassination," Viola flicked the penultimate lever and eyed the final toggle in the middle of the panel.

Mr Chester turned to Viola. The light tube cast long shadows over his face, shading his eyes and extending his brows over his forehead. "Step away, now."

"I thought you were in Her Majesty's employ?" asked Viola.

"I work for the good of the Empire," he replied. "And this machine could prove a valuable resource in its service."

"You said you would help me exonerate Sir Archibald," Viola's fingers nails dug into her palms. "You promised. One day, you said."

"Circumstances have changed. I can't allow you to meddle with the machine."

"You can always confiscate Professor Black's research notes. I'm sure they will contain all the technical specifications required."

"I already have them," Mr Chester smiled, "which is why I still want the machine. With a bit of work, our scientists could make it–"

A low grinding tumbled down from the ceiling. The walls vibrated, filling the room with a ghost-like moaning.

"The machine?" hissed Mr Chester. "What have you done?"

Viola took a deep breath. For the Queen. She snapped the final toggle in position. And for you, Archie. She twisted the calendar dial to its limit - 1.9.9.9. She stepped back from the pedestal and watched the brass rings spin, with a gentle, hypnotic swish. It was done.

The rings spun faster and faster until they whined in protest. The Chronosphere trembled. Spurts of steam trickled from its base and seeped through the edges of the wooden wall panels.

Mr Chester stormed toward the pedestal and slammed the toggle back to its original position. The rings blurred. Puffs of grey smoke plunged into the spinning sphere of metal and disintegrated into the air.

"What have you done!" he growled. "We need that prototype."

Viola snatched up the carpet bag and stepped away from the pedestal.

He ran his hand over the panel. "There must be another switch." There was a loud click. He grinned.

The floor rumbled under their feet. The far wall shivered. One end disengaged from the side wall and scraped forward several feet. The floor shuddered.

Viola grabbed the edge of the pedestal to regain her balance. She met Mr Chester's gaze. There was a hint of panic in his eyes.

The room turned slowly clockwise, taking the far wall with it, concealing the other half of the room, and the laboratory door, behind it. They were trapped.

Machinery screamed beneath them. The room turned one hundred and eighty degrees. The blank wall was gone. In its place was a wall, with a duplicate door, complete with a ticking grandfather clock next to it.

Viola stared at the wall. The room had moved. The mechanics alone would be... She blinked. The. Room. Had. Moved. She stumbled forward, clutching the carpet bag to her chest. She fumbled at the doorknob. The door opened into the front hallway. Mrs Whitehead was gone. Had she escaped? Viola glanced along the hall. The front door hung at an odd angle. The curiosity cabinet stood on one side, an Oriental vase sat on the hall table on the other. But that was broken when...

"Two front halls?"

"And a duplicate street through the back door." Mr Chester was by her side.

"It's all counterfeit?" she asked.

Footsteps hurried along the hall toward them. Mr Chester lifted his light tube, revealing Sir Archibald and–

"Henry!" Viola ran up to him and threw her arms around him.

He hugged her and turned his head toward the rumbling noise. His muscles stiffened.

"What's wrong?" she whispered.

"Chester." Henry stepped back from Viola, his hand still clasping hers. "I wondered where you'd gotten to."

She turned to Sir Archibald. "The Chronosphere is counterfeit. The

Professor is a fraud."

"I know," he replied.

"We have to leave." Viola moved toward the door and tugged at Henry's hand.

He didn't move.

"Henry?"

He released her hand.

Viola glanced at Mr Chester and back to Henry. "There's no time for posturing," she said.

Both men stood their ground.

A rumbling roar blasted the laboratory. The walls shuddered. Shards of metal embedded themselves into the wall behind Mr Chester. Smoke belched into the hall.

Viola grabbed Henry's hand. "I suggest we run."

The crisp scent of pine filled the air. Frosted tips sparkled on mistletoe sprigs hanging from the ceiling.

"I love Christmas," said Viola. "It reminds me of home. Father would always choose the tallest tree. Sometimes it was so tall the tip would bend over." She giggled. "And it was impossible to put the angel on top."

"We never had a tree when I was a boy." Paper rustled as Sir Archibald draped a paper chain over a bough.

"Then you shall have the honour of placing the angel when we're done." Viola clipped a miniature candle onto a branch of the tree. It jiggled; reflected gaslight danced on the ceiling. "Everything is so ...shiny." She sighed. "Anne and I used to take turns–" Viola caught her breath. The silver clip snapped her finger and the candle fell to the floor.

"You can't keep blaming yourself," whispered Sir Archibald.

Viola's wiped a tear from her cheek as she bent down to retrieve the candle. "You're correct." Viola took a deep breath. "I must live for the future, not dwell in the past."

She glanced in Henry's direction. He stood silently by the fire, arranging handmade Christmas cards amongst the holly trimming along the mantelpiece. His waistcoat peeked out from under his unbuttoned jacket - blue with a delicately stitched gold pattern. Viola smiled. It fit perfectly; A few weeks without Polly's chocolate cake had its benefits.

"Have you told him about Scotland?" asked Sir Archibald.

"Best not. He'll just worry. I was supposed to be recuperating."

"Secrets already?" Sir Archibald tsked. "And you're not even married yet."

Viola straightened one of the candles, avoiding his gaze.

"And will you tell him you were tricked by Professor Black and almost blackmailed by the The Society?"

"Not I." He picked up a piece of orange from the delicious morsels Polly had left on the table beside a jug of eggnog. "Besides, I've signed the Secrets Act."

"And Mr Chester said he will keep our names out of the report if I allow him to take credit for Mrs Whitehead's capture." Viola eyed the assortment of candied fruits on the tray, crusted with spots of sugar. She selected the last piece of fig and popped it into her mouth.

Sir Archibald chuckled. "Henry was eyeing the figs."

"Perhaps that's why he's sulking?" she said.

"He's doesn't want to attend Lady Calthorpe's party," Sir Archibald replied.

"Why ever not?" asked Viola.

Sir Archibald lowered his voice. "She keeps asking about the wedding. He doesn't know how to answer."

"Oh." Poor Henry. She hadn't thought her reluctance to set a date would have such repercussions.

"You should tell him how you feel, Viola." he whispered.

"But-" Viola clasped her hands.

"He'll surprise you." He patted her shoulder. "Live for the future, remember?"

Viola nodded, dusted grains of sugar from her bodice and joined Henry by the fireplace.

"We'll need to order a carriage if we are to arrive in time for Lady Calthorpe's party," said Henry.

"Do you mind if we send our apologies?" She put her hand on his arm. "I've had too much excitement for one day."

"Are you certain?" Henry took her hand in his.

"I'm sure she will understand." Viola gazed into his bright blue eyes. Her heart fluttered. How could she have *ever* been distracted by the likes of Mr Chester?

"Excellent. I prefer small parties." Sir Archibald clapped his hands. "I've got a present for you, Viola." He pulled a brown paper package from behind a chair and presented it to her.

Viola slipped off the patterned ribbon, opened one end of the parcel and slipped out the contents - a magazine and a new copy of *A Christmas Carol.*

"I noticed your copy was getting worn," said Sir Archibald, "and I thought it fitting - ghosts of Christmas future, past, and all."

"And the magazine?" asked Henry.

"It's the story I promised Viola," replied Sir Archibald, "by that young writer I told you about, Bertie Wells."

Viola grinned.

"I have a present for you as well, Vi." Henry's eyes twinkled; he pressed a small parcel into her hands.

Viola unwrapped it: a decoratively-tooled purple leather journal with gilt-edged pages. Her name was embossed, in gold, on the front cover. A leather strap, with a fine gold lock, held it shut.

"It's a secret journal," said Henry, "to record your adventures." He dropped a small key on a chain, into her palm. "Only you have the key."

Viola's heart fluttered. It was the perfect gift. She hugged him. "I love you, Henry Collins."

The clock on the mantelpiece clicked. Sir Archibald held his breath. Viola counted the chimes: ... Ten. Eleven. Twelve.

Sir Archibald relaxed and smiled at her. "A toast?"

Viola picked up her cup of eggnog. "To being alive."

THE END

The Illusioneer

Chapter 1: Promise

The limelights hissed and flared into life as the audience dribbled into the hall. Boots clacked on the wooden floors. The echoes of voices faded as the hall filled, coalescing into a background murmur.

Viola wove her way through the crowded aisle, around huddled clusters of eager on-lookers jostling for the best seats. She paused, waiting for Henry to catch up - and to avoid catching Lady Calthorpe's eye. She had been particularly attentive to Viola's state of affairs since Christmas. Too attentive.

Viola stepped into the shadow of a rotund gentleman, deep in conversation with his friend. She glanced over the man's shoulder at occupied seats in the front row. Lady Calthorpe would be there - no doubt - keeping watch on the aisle, having secured front row seats for both Viola and Henry next to her and Lord Calthorpe.

Rank had its privilege, and Lady Calthorpe was always offered the prerogative to exercise that privilege. Viola bit her lip. That was unkind; Lady Calthorpe had every right to her privileges. There were few women who would not accept such concessions, nor welcome respect from the male establishment.

Warm fingers wrapped around Viola's hand. She turned to see Henry's brilliant blue eyes smiling at her.

"Tell me again, why are we here?" she asked.

"I thought I'd present you with an alternative detectiving challenge.

One less perilous than your usual exploits." He winked at her.

Viola sighed. "You know what I think about hypnotists, Henry. Poking around in someone's subconscious will only lead to no good." It was a woolly science at best, outright quackery at worst.

"Then see if you can solve how the trick is done. The Mighty Alessandro is supposed to be the fastest hypnotist in London. His record is twenty subjects at one assembly." He patted her on the hand. "And it could be fun."

"Fun?" Viola raised an eyebrow.

Henry nodded in the direction of the front row. "Lady Calthorpe is here."

Viola turned to face the stage. Lady Calthorpe beamed from under a massive orange bonnet; its feathers jiggled as she waved them forward.

"Doesn't she know it's all just an act?"

Henry shook his head. "She's been talking about it for days. I do hope they ask for volunteers. She would not hesitate to offer up herself as a subject, if given the chance." His moustache twitched. "Wouldn't you adore seeing her cluck like a chicken?"

Viola tugged her hand free from his grip. "Henry, don't be so cruel." She slapped him on his wrist. "Lady Calthorpe is a very generous woman and is always willing to offer support." She leaned closer to Henry. "They don't pick subjects at random; they only use paid volunteers placed amongst the audience. And Lady Calthorpe would never agree to humiliate herself in front of society and friends."

Henry's moustache drooped. "You can be a stick-in-the-mud, sometimes."

"I don't want to encourage them."

"Them?"

"Charlatans and fraudsters, like this Alessandro."

"Perhaps their methods could be useful. There have been some studies in France. A doctor there has postulated its use to manage patients in the asylum."

A gaggle of socialites squeezed past them. Viola grabbed her skirt and tucked it behind her.

"He also said hypnotism was a manifestation of hysteria," whispered Viola.

"Ah." Henry waved on the socialites' top-hatted companions.

"And I suppose you believe in fairies as well?" asked Viola.

Henry dropped his gaze.

Lady Calthorpe beckoned them closer and patted the seat next to her. Lord Calthorpe closed his eyes and took a deep breath. Viola and Henry made their way toward the front seats.

"Do we have to...?"

"No," replied Henry. "But we should. Lady Calthorpe did invite us."

Viola examined Lady Calthorpe's enthusiastic face. Her cheeks were blushing and her eyes sparkled. Viola would never hear the end of it if she absconded. She took a deep breath and edged past a tall gentleman standing at the end of the front row of seats. Henry followed her along the row.

Lady Calthorpe jumped to her feet. "Doctor Stewart, you came! And you brought Doctor Collins. Excellent. Do sit."

Henry leaned forward and shook Lord Calthorpe's hand. "Congratulations on your appointment as Commander of Windsor Sky Cannon and Armoury. Her Majesty will be in good hands."

Viola nodded, settled into the leather chair and straightened her skirts. She glanced in the direction of the stage. Shadows bobbed up into the light as the stage hands skittered around the front of the stage. One remained at the foot of each light fixture.

The stage curtains twitched. The hall lights dimmed. The drone of the crowd hushed. A crack appeared in the centre of the heavy curtains; its corners lifted and peeled apart to reveal a tall, black-clad man, his face hidden in the shadow of his top hat. He extended his hand toward the audience; his cloak hugged his arm, revealing a brilliant ruby-red lining.

Violin music wafted up from the orchestra pit.

The man stepped forward. The gathered curtains dropped behind him with a soft thud. He lifted his chin and smiled. The stage lights brightened, until they glinted off his cravat pin.

"Good evening, ladies and gentlemen." His deep voice rolled over the audience like a wave.

Lady Calthorpe gasped and clutched her purse.

Viola slipped her arm around Henry's elbow. She'd hate to see Lady Calthorpe hoodwinked into an unfortunate situation.

"I require a volunteer from the audience," Alessandro continued. "But only those intelligent few, whose minds are open to new possibilities, will be able to attain a true hypnotic state."

A buzz ran through the crowd. Viola tugged on Henry's arm. Here we go.

Lady Calthorpe shifted in her seat. Viola's heart sank. Lady Calthorpe would be disappointed when The Mighty Alessandro was exposed for what he really was.

Alessandro stepped forward, near the edge of the stage and surveyed the willing crowd. His long finger crooked in the direction of the Calthorpes.

"You, sir. You look like a strong-willed gentleman."

Viola's gaze followed the direction in which he pointed. Her eye widened. Lord Calthorpe? She clasped Henry's arm with her free hand. Not a paid volunteer? Something was afoot.

Lord Calthorpe glanced at the row behind him and back to the stage. "Me?" he whispered.

"Yes, you, Herbert." Lady Calthorpe patted her husband's hand. "Go on, dear." The sparkle had faded from her eyes.

"Perhaps he shall choose you next, my dear?"

Lord Calthorpe stood slowly and ascended the steps to the stage.

"Good evening, sir," said Alessandro.

"Lord Calthorpe," he corrected.

Alessandro bowed his head and smiled. "Welcome, Your Lordship, to my humble display of enchantment."

A faint whirring emitted from inside Lord Calthorpe's glove. He slipped his hand into his pocket and nodded. Viola frowned. His mechanical hand sometimes had a mind of its own, particularly when he was nervous. Alessandro clasped Lord Calthorpe's free hand in his and whispered in his ear. Lord Calthorpe's eyes widened. Alessandro released Lord Calthorpe's hand and circled around him, until his back was to the audience.

"What is he saying?" asked Viola.

Lady Calthorpe reached into her purse, pulled out her spectacles and slipped them on. She peered onto the stage. Viola leaned forward and turned her ear toward the stage, trying to hear the conversation but, even in the hushed hall, she heard nothing.

Lord Calthorpe nodded, removed his now-silent hand from his pocket and snapped to attention. He stared into the audience - motionless. Alessandro waved his hand in front of Lord Calthorpe's face. He didn't blink; his eyes remained fixed on an unseen spot before him. Alessandro's cloak swirled as he motioned to the side of the stage, and turned toward the audience.

"Ladies and gentlemen, let me now demonstrate the power of hypnotism. His Lordship is now in a deep trance."

Assistants brought in two chairs and positioned them on either side of Lord Calthorpe, their backs facing him. One of the assistants stepped behind him.

"Ladies and gentleman, I assure you there is no risk to His Lordship." Alessandro nudged Lord Calthorpe's chest. His rigid body fell backwards.

Lady Calthorpe's knuckles paled as she gripped her purse tighter.

The assistant caught Lord Calthorpe's shoulder. The second assistant scooped up his feet. They lifted him and rested his rigid body across the chairs. Alessandro twirled with a flourish and bowed as the assistants returned Lord Calthorpe to his feet. Alessandro placed his hand on Lord Calthorpe's forehead and snapped it away again. Lord Calthorpe's shoulders relaxed. His eyelids flickered.

"Welcome back, Your Lordship."

Viola raised an eyebrow. The audience clapped as he was led to the edge of the stage. Whispers filled the hall. Lord Calthorpe shuffled back to his place and lowered himself onto his seat.

Alessandro flipped his cape back over his shoulder. "I require another volunteer."

The audience quietened.

Viola leaned closer. "What did he say to you?"

Lord Calthorpe shrugged. "Nothing."

"Curious." Henry raised an eyebrow.

"That's not the word I would use for it," said Viola.

"It seems we have a sceptic in the audience." Alessandro smiled. "Please let me persuade you otherwise, dear lady."

Henry nudged Viola. She nudged him back.

"It's you, Vi," said Henry.

Lady Calthorpe sighed and dropped her hands in her lap. "You go, dear. It will be amusing."

Amusing? A cold shiver flitted over Viola's body. She shook her head. It wasn't amusing when her mother had engaged such charlatans. Nor was it amusing when she cried herself to sleep. No good could come of this.

Henry leaned close and whispered in her ear. "Here's your chance, Vi."

"But, Henry... "

"Show him for what he is," Henry grinned.

Viola rose slowly from her chair and approached the stage steps. She would show him up for the charlatan he was. She wrapped her fingers around the railing; her boot heel thunked on the bottom step. She hesitated. Her mother had frequented spiritualists and mesmerists, bewitched with the idea of finding Anne. It had proved fruitless - at least to her mother; its only bounty was that which lined the swindlers' pockets. They led her on, each one a fraud. It all led to nothing but disappointment. Her mother had never been the same again.

Viola's heart thumped. She gripped the railing and strode up the steps. She had no idea how Lord Calthorpe had been hoodwinked into compliance, but she was determined. She would show The Mighty Alessandro for what he was: a fake.

He removed his hat, strode toward her, hand extended; an ornate ring glittered in the light. He grinned. His cape billowed behind him. "Good evening, Miss...?"

"Doctor Stewart," replied Viola, clasping her hands together.

Alessandro nodded and lowered his hand. Piano keys tinkled. A violin joined in.

"A doctor?" His smile slipped, then returned with a vengeance. "You look nervous, Doctor Stewart." He laughed. "No need to worry, dear lady. Hypnotism only works on those who want to be hypnotised. Perhaps it's the thrill of doing something and getting away with it, when you can't be held responsible for your own actions."

She glanced back at Lord Calthorpe; he hadn't moved. She swallowed. *Mother had been obsessed.* Viola took a deep breath. What had Alessandro said? *It only works on those who want to be hypnotised.* Well, she did *not* wish to be. She exhaled slowly, allowing her body to relax, and stepped forward.

"Tell me, Doctor Stewart, what are you doing later this evening? Dinner with friends?"

Viola nodded. She and Henry were meeting Sir Archibald for dinner at The Langham. Light reflected off Alessandro's cravat pin and danced as he glided around her.

"Tell me, Doctor Stewart, do your hands feel heavy?"

Viola shook her head. He slipped in front of the light. She squinted, struggling to see his face clearly against the blazing limelight. A feathery halo surrounded his head where his hat had been. He stepped closer and stared into her eye.

Mother had been hoodwinked by charlatans.

"Are your eyelids heavy?"

Viola blinked. She glanced into the audience, searching for Henry in the sea of dark shadows, beyond the limelight. Their gentle hiss cushioned his voice. Her cheeks flushed under their heat. She swallowed. Her reply caught in her throat.

"Have you ever been on a holiday at the beach?" he asked. "Was it a happy time?"

Viola nodded.

"Do you remember the sand? Hot. Relaxing." He stepped closer. "And can you hear the waves? Remember the relaxing sound of water lapping on the pebbles."

He placed a gentle hand on her shoulder. A warmth spread across her body and down her arms. Her shoulders dropped.

"Taste the salt."

Viola licked her lips.

His voice hummed, mingling with the sound of the lights. Shadows rolled over the audience, crawled up the stage and swallowed the lights.

Mother had never been the same...

Dinner had been superb. Viola could still smell the mouth-watering aroma of the roast meats, and taste the sweet pastries. She closed her eye and listened to the rhythm of the Brougham cab's iron-rimmed wheels as they clattered on the cobblestones: clickety clack, clickety clack. She tapped her toe to the beat. She turned her face toward the window. The cool air was crisp and clear - no fog to bind the city stench to the street.

Viola's breaths slowed. She felt as though a weight had been lifted from her. Was this how contentment felt?

She opened her eye and drank in Henry's visage. His suit jacket was unbuttoned. Flashes of purple damask waistcoat winked at her as the carriage jiggled over the uneven streets. A lock of dark hair fell over his forehead. Her heart skipped. Henry stared out the window, seemingly oblivious to her attention.

Viola leaned forward, placed her hand on Henry's and smiled. He slipped his hand away from hers and leaned back into the leather seat of the carriage.

"Did you mean what you said at dinner?" he asked.

"Hmm...?" Viola leaned back into her seat and frowned. She had little recollection of the dinner conversation; she remembered only that it had been as convivial as the food had been delicious. Perhaps she'd had too much wine? "About what, Henry?"

Deep furrows burrowed into his forehead. "Did you mean it?"

Viola sat bolt upright and stared at him. "Henry, this isn't like you." He avoided her gaze. "Why are you angry with me?" she asked.

Henry yanked up the carriage window, with a snap. "Don't play games, Viola."

Her heart sank. She'd never seen Henry so furious. She tried to recount the evening but it was a muffled blur.

"Please, Henry. I have no idea what you are talking about."

Henry closed his eyes, took a deep breath, and opened them slowly. He stared in her direction - not at her, but past her. Viola's chest tightened.

What had she done?

"Sir Archibald is a close friend, but..." He buttoned up his jacket. "You could at least have done me the courtesy to have revealed your feelings in private." Henry lowered his gaze. "To give me time to digest such unexpected revelations." He clenched his hands.

Viola's mind raced, trying to recollect the evening's events: They'd met Lord and Lady Calthorpe at the hall. Lord Calthorpe had been hypnotised, then herself. Then they'd... She searched her memory. They'd had dinner. Yes, that was it. She and Henry had met Sir Archibald for dinner at The Langham, and then...

She licked her lips. They tasted of salt. She remembered water lapping on pebbles. The Mighty Alessandro? What had he said to her? She held her breath. Relax? Yes. *Relax and hear my voice. Relax and tell the truth.*

"Henry, please, what did I say?" she asked.

Henry's voice was barely a whisper. "If you truly do not wish to be married to me then—"

"But I do!" Viola slid to the edge of the seat. "I *do* want to marry you, Henry Collins."

"That is not what you told Sir Archibald."

Relax and tell the truth. Viola swallowed. Had the hypnotism worked? She shook her head. A chill trickled along her veins. Impossible!

"It was Alessandro. He—"

"Made you say it?" Henry's moustache twitched. "It only works on those who want to be hypnotised, Viola." Henry slouched back into his seat.

"I love you, Henry, and I do want to marry you."

"Then why the delay?

"I should have spoken of it earlier. Sir Archibald told me—"

Henry's eyes widened. "Archie knew?" Henry growled.

"He guessed." Viola edged back into her seat. "He begged me to tell you, but there was never an opportune time.”

“An opportune time?” Henry’s moustache drooped.

“Henry, I *do* want to marry you.” Viola spoke slowly, contemplating each word before she spoke, “But my heart is not entirely mine to give.”

Henry’s muscles tensed.

“It’s Anne.” Viola gripped the edge of the seat. “It was my fault my sister ran away. It broke our mother’s heart and left a hole in mine. And, until I discover her fate, my heart is not my own to give, and could never be entirely yours either.”

Henry folded his arms and stared out the carriage window.

“Henry?”

He remained silent.

The trickle in Viola’s veins became a torrent. A chilled wave enveloped her body.

The carriage jolted as it rounded the corner into Greater Marylebone Street and shuddered to a halt in front of Viola’s house.

“Are you coming in, Henry?” she asked.

“Not tonight, Viola,” He avoided her gaze.

Viola stepped onto the footpath. The door clicked shut behind her; the carriage clattered on the cobblestones and turned into High Street.

Viola trudged along the path toward the Bird Walk. Pebbles crunched underfoot. She paused at the Parrot Enclosure. Sun glinted on the polished metal bars. Birds trilled and whistled and flitted in their cages. Trapped. Unable to fly free. Viola’s chest tightened. She felt trapped, as they were.

A parrot strutted closer along a naked branch, twitched its head and eyed her through the bars. And freedom. She stopped by its cage. It buried its beak into its colourful plumage and fixed an eye on her. She frowned. The poor bird looked so forlorn. Perhaps it was better to not know what lies beyond one's confines? Perhaps it was best to live in ignorance and not want for more?

Footsteps crunched behind her. Sir Archibald hurried along the path to meet her, nodded in greeting.

"I came as soon as I could." Sir Archibald surveyed the buildings. An elephant trumpeted in the nearby enclosure. "An interesting choice for a rendezvous."

"I had to get out and clear my head." Viola's heart sank into her stomach. "Henry refuses to see me." Viola felt the colour drain from her face. "What have I done?"

"You look pale, Viola. You should sit down." Sir Archibald rested his hand on her elbow.

She shook her head. "What *did* I say, last night?"

"You mentioned your holiday in Scotland, sea bathing and..." Sir Archibald pushed his spectacles up his nose. "And Mr Chester."

Why couldn't she remember? Viola's head spun. What must Henry think of her? She leaned against the bars of the cage. Was he jealous?

"Nothing happened," she whispered.

"I'm sure Henry knows that." Sir Archibald cleared his throat. "But, Viola, you should have told him about Mr Chester, and his proposition, when you returned from Scotland."

"Why? He doesn't own me." She clicked her tongue to get the bird's attention. The parrot edged closer. "I can speak with whomever I wish."

"It's a matter of trust," said Sir Archibald.

"Yes, but..." Viola twisted the engagement ring on her finger.

"You wanted him to trust you. Well, it works both ways."

Viola stuck her finger into the cage and beckoned the bird closer.

"You, my dear, are in the enviable position of holding another's heart in your hands. You own it. But be careful, hearts are fragile."

Viola grasped the bars of the cage. "What about my heart? My trust?"

"Have you not noticed how hard he is trying to prove he trusts you, Viola? You asked him to leave you to your detectiving. He did so - even when you take unnecessary risks."

Viola gripped the bars tighter. "I do not—"

The bird squawked and flapped its wings against the wire mesh of its cage. Downy feathers wafted in the air. A sharp pain seared through Viola's knuckle. She snapped her hand away from the cage and spun on her heel to face Sir Archibald. Blood beaded on her skin.

"Oh, you don't?" Sir Archibald raised an eyebrow. "You two are more alike than you realise."

Viola sucked her finger. Sir Archibald smiled and handed her a handkerchief.

"Henry thinks you don't trust him, Viola."

"But I *do* trust him."

"Don't tell me. Tell him." His voice was calm. "He's shown he trusts you - even though he's worried you'll be hurt - because you asked him to. Now you need to do the same."

"But he won't talk to me." She placed her hand on Sir Archibald's arm.

"His pride is injured, Viola."

His pride? Viola scoffed. "What about my pride? What about my heart? Is a woman's heart worth any less than a man's?"

"Of course not." Sir Archibald patted her hand. "But it is eminently stronger."

Viola's breathing faltered. "Am I too late?" She struggled to breathe. "Does he still love me?"

"Of course he does," replied Sir Archibald. "He doesn't have a choice. But he thinks you don't want him."

"I *do*, but..." Viola twisted the engagement ring on her finger. "I... I can't, not yet. It wouldn't be fair to him. I can't give my entire heart until I find..." The words stuck in her throat. Pain radiated through her chest, into her neck and shoulder.

"Your sister?"

Viola nodded.

"He can't compete with her memory." Sir Archibald took her arm in his and led her away from the Parrot Enclosure, toward the Elephant House. "Just give Henry time to recover."

Viola hesitated, forcing Sir Archibald to a halt. She took a deep breath. "What about my recovery?"

"That will be difficult," replied Sir Archibald, "if you don't let go of the past, my dear."

"We've had this conversation before," said Viola.

Sir Archibald nodded. "Yes, we have. And you can't delay it any longer."

Footsteps skipped toward them. Two girls with bouncing pigtails giggled as they hurried past Viola and Sir Archibald.

Sir Archibald lowered his voice: "You need to make a decision, my dear: the past or the future."

Viola scuffed the toe of her boot into the gravel and avoided Sir Archibald's gaze. He patted her hand and escorted her toward a knot of cavorting children waiting their turn for a ride on the tamed pachyderm.

"You need a holiday," he said. "A few months to let Henry lick his wounds - and to get some colour back into your cheeks. Perhaps a tour of Europe? See the sights? You could visit the Eiffel Tower."

"Is it really as monstrous as they say?"

"Why don't you tell me?" Sir Archibald smiled. "Use the time to do something you love. Have an adventure. I'm sure Europe has many mysteries worthy of Doctor Viola Stewart."

"Without a chaperone?" Viola gasped sarcastically and giggled. The children's laughter was contagious. "Lady Calthorpe would be shocked."

"I'm sure young Polly would love to accompany you." They strode toward the Elephant House. "She deserves a holiday as well."

"We could take the Channel Airship Service to Paris...," said Viola.

"I shall write to my friend, Professor Algernon Woolington. He teaches at the School of Medicine in Paris. His wife is a physicist, studied in Edinburgh. Definitely not conventional. You'll get along famously." He paused mid-step and frowned. "But they're going to Venice for Carnevale." He grinned. "A party is just what you need."

Viola eyed Sir Archibald. She was being *organised*. She wondered if Lady Calthorpe had had a hand in it all. They stopped near the enclosure gates.

"Go. Enjoy yourself," whispered Sir Archibald, "make your decision, and put Henry out of his misery on your return - one way or the other."

Viola watched the children as they jostled to be first in line. A top-hatted gentleman waved a ticket in the air. A zookeeper nodded and took the hand of a small boy and led him toward a brightly painted step next to the elephant. They were happy, untouched by the troubles and responsibilities of the world. Carefree. She'd forgotten how that felt. She sighed. Perhaps she could forget her guilt? Perhaps Henry could...

Viola's pulse raced. "What if Henry still refuses to see me?"

"I'll take care of Henry," replied Sir Archibald.

Henry stared out of the window of the departure tower. The muted cry of gulls surrounded them. A freshly-painted dirigible bobbed at the end of its tether. Sunlight glinted off a row of portholes lining the edge of the hull. Soot-stained men scuttled around on a platform around the hull of the dirigible, pulled lines taut and secured them to over-sized brass mooring bollards.

A rope unravelled and snapped in the direction of one of the workers.

Polly gasped behind Henry. One of the handles of her large, red carpet bag slipped from her grasp and swung loose in her hand.

Henry clenched his hands and stepped in front of Viola. "Are you sure it's safe?" he asked.

"They've made considerable improvements," Viola replied, her eyes fixed on the flying machine. "Or so I'm told."

A stocky gentleman, with prominent muttonchops and expensive top hat, sauntered past them. A burly attendant followed him closely. The gentleman's ticket dangled from his fingers as he lit his cigar. Its end flared red; the paper ticket fluttered in his hand - too close for comfort - as he paused by the window.

Henry's muscles tensed. He glanced at the gas-filled dirigible, back at the gentleman, and finally to Viola. It wasn't safe for her to travel with such a careless fool. Viola fidgeted with her purse, her gaze following a ring of smoke rising around the gentleman's head.

Henry took her arm. He wanted to implore her not to travel, but it was not his decision. "Viola, I—"

A ticket collector stepped forward, snatched the gentleman's ticket and pointed to the prominent sign on the wall near the tower entrance. Its red letters demanded:

NO NAKED FLAMES.
NO SPARKS.
NO EMBERS.
By Order of
The Channel Airship Service

He held out his hand, presented a small, octagonal container to the gentleman and flipped open its lid. The gentleman raised an eyebrow, stubbed out his cigar and deposited it in the container. The ticket collector nodded stiffly, snapped the lid closed and marched back to his booth.

Henry felt Viola's arm muscles relax. He let out a slow breath.

"Her Majesty had good reason to ban airships from our skies, you know, Viola," he said.

Viola eyed the dirigible. "I know. I was there," she whispered. "I saw it fall."

Henry's moustache drooped. "I didn't know." Viola had never spoken of it before: the turning point in The Empire's laws on mechanical ownership. And she chose to reveal such an incident now, as she was preparing to abandon him for months of adventure in Europe? He felt ill. Had he lost her already? He hugged Viola's arm. "Are you sure you—?"

"I need to go, Henry." She smiled, removed his arm from hers and moved closer to the window, never taking her attention from the floating transport, as it bobbed in the sea winds. Polly clutched the carpetbag to her chest, bobbed in Henry's direction and followed Viola.

Henry's hand twitched. He wanted to hold her hand, to comfort her. He watched her press up against the window. The floating transport nudged the tower. He clenched his hand. Viola's eye widened. She seemed so excited, yet the tone in her voice suggested concern. He stretched his fingers and eyed the airship. If she was concerned about it falling to a fiery death, she hid her emotions well. As with so many other things... His heart thumped. He searched her face, looking for any clue to her thoughts.

The shadow of the dirigible glided across her cornea. He watched the gleam in her eye left in its wake. He held his breath, trying to slow his heart beat. He wanted her to stay. He wanted to protect her from danger, from her own curiosity. But then the gleam would fade. She had asked him to allow her time to find the answers she needed. He'd promised. Now it was his turn to trust her.

Cogs groaned. Steam hissed as it escaped from the engines. The walkway rumbled and ratcheted out from the tower, toward the door of the dirigible. The workmen secured it to the hull and waved back to the tower.

Viola turned to face Henry, batted her lashes and smiled. "Time to go."

The ticket collector took his place as the tower door opened. A chill breeze caught Viola's hair. Soft tendrils caressed her face.

Henry's lip flickered, managing a weak smile. If only he knew she would return... He took a deep breath.

He reached for her hand. "Promise me you'll have a safe journey." His heart thumped quicker. "And come home." He squeezed Viola's hand gently.

Viola gazed into his eyes. "My dear Henry, as if I had a choice?"

Henry kissed her hand. "And try to keep out of trouble."

Viola smiled and strolled toward the departure door.

The private dirigible compartment resembled that of a first-class train. A narrow table of dark, inlaid wood sat between the high-back bench-seats of carved wood and teal velvet upholstery. Plump cushions lined the seats and leaned against the hull. In place of sash windows, three brass-edged portholes - almost two feet in diameter - pierced the hull, providing scenic views of the countryside below.

Wisps of cloud drifted and curled past the portholes. The sky was a brilliant clear blue, no sign of the grey fog that often muddied the London sky. Beads of moisture condensed on the glass. Viola tapped her fingertip on the pane. It was cold. How high were they travelling? She twisted the latch, opened the window a crack and took a deep breath.

The smell was... She sniffed again. There was no smell; no city stench, no lingering smell of rubbish-filled alleyways, nor over-crowded decaying tenements. The only rookeries here would be populated by birds, not people.

A flurry of wind rushed through the opening, bringing with it the rhythmic chug of the steam engines. Polly grinned and leapt up onto the seat under the far porthole. She knelt on a velvet cushion and dangled her feet off the edge of the seat, jiggled her ankles in excitement and stared at the view through the porthole.

Viola grinned. Polly's enthusiasm reminded her of her own first dirigible encounter, as a child. Father had bought her a flying toy: a steam-powered concoction of lace and ribbons, with a wooden control box. She remembered the trickles of smoke that swirled as it moved. She could almost hear the thunk it made when it bumped into a lady's bonnet. She bit her lip, trying not to laugh, and smiled. And remembered the scowl of the man who confiscated it. She caught her breath. The man who'd used it to sabotage...

Viola closed her eye, trying to quell the ghostly screams of those who had perished. Her lungs felt as if they would explode. She'd never forget that day. She squeezed a velvet cushion to her chest. *Never*.

"Everything looks so tiny." Polly squealed with delight.

Viola opened her eye. Polly's cheek pressed against the glass as she wriggled to get a better view below them. Viola stared silently out of the window; her fingernails dug into her palm.

Golden ribbons flared toward the horizon and twisted upward to rim the clouds with their glow. The ribbons coalesced, changing colour from a delicious pale toffee, to tangerine then saffron. They watched the sun sink below the clouds. The sky darkened.

A chill crept into the compartment. Viola shivered and closed the porthole window. Polly grinned, reached into the carpetbag and pulled out a neatly folded package and untied the string.

Viola raised an eyebrow. "I wondered what you packed in there?"

"Only the travelling essentials," replied Polly. "I heard it gets chilly at high altitude, so I packed a warm travel coat." Polly held up a purple woollen *visite*, intricately embroidered in pearlescent silk. Tufts of Arctic fox trim peeked out from the cuffs and collar.

Viola's lungs relaxed. "What would I do without you, Polly?"

Polly's grin faded. She slumped onto the seat and, as if suddenly remembering her Mistress was present, straightened to attention and plumped up the cushion beside her.

"I apologise, Miss." She avoided eye contact. "It's just..." She straightened the skirts of her new bustle gown.

"Is there something wrong?" Viola's heart sank. Perhaps she had overheard Henry's concerns about the safety of air travel. "Doctor Collins was worrying over nothing." She sat in the seat opposite Polly. "Air travel is quite safe." Viola straightened her skirts. It had to be.

"It's not—" Polly shook her head. "It's the dress, Miss..."

"Is it not to your liking?" Viola sighed. "Perhaps we should have purchased the green?"

"No, Miss, the dress is beautiful, but..." Her voice dropped to a whisper. "But it's worth a month's wages. I couldn't afford to pay you back if—" Polly winced. "When we return to London..." There was pain in Polly's eyes. "When you take up new residence... I suppose you will require a change in staffing arrangements?"

Viola nodded. It was a logical assumption. "There's no hurry." Viola shifted in her seat.

Polly cleared her throat, her words spilled out, like a full speed train: "Miss, am I to be let go when we return to London? Is all this to be compensation?" Polly twisted the hem of her overskirt.

Viola snapped to attention. "Oh no, Polly. I could never let you go." She leaned forward and took Polly's hand in hers. "How could I? You've been with me since I was a child. Your mother was my governess. I trust you more than anyone else."

"Even more than Doctor Collins?"

Viola didn't reply.

Viola squeezed Polly's hand. "You will always have a place in my household, even if my situation should change."

"*If*, Miss?" Polly frowned. "Are you not going to marry Doctor Collins?"

Viola noted a hint of concern in Polly's voice. The poor girl must be terrified for her future.

"No need to worry, Polly." Viola patted her hand. "Of course, I'll marry Doctor Collins."

Viola felt Polly's hand relax beneath hers.

Eventually.

The supper trolley rattled along the passageway outside their compartment. Viola's stomach grumbled. It had been ages since afternoon tea.

"Ah, that will be supper," said Viola. "I'm famished."

Polly pushed the service button, opened the door and searched the passageway.

"There's no-one here," she said. "The trolley is moving by itself."

Viola looked into the passageway. The trolley's wheels sat in a metal track running the length of the passage. It trundled closer and halted outside their compartment door.

Steam swirled around inside the rectangular glass dome covering the tray; heat radiated from the glass, warming her face. Viola inspected the contents of the trolley: roast quail with asparagus and mushrooms - Henry's favourite - on a polished, silver plate.

Polly pressed a button. Gears clicked inside the trolley. A panel opened and a tray rolled out. The aroma of freshly cooked mushrooms filled the compartment. Viola licked her lips and tried not to think of Henry.

Chapter 2: Deception

The door of the Ascension Chamber unfolded and clicked shut. The chamber quivered. Viola shivered, wrapped her fingers around the handrail on the wall beside her and glanced around the metal cage.

The tall operator in a Channel Airship Service Company uniform rattled the door, flipped the latch and pushed down on the control lever. Cogs whirred and machinery groaned. The chamber lurched and began its descent.

Viola shut her eye and gripped the bar tighter. She doubted she would ever become comfortable in the claustrophobic enclosures. Her ears buzzed, muffling the voices of fellow passengers behind her, rendering them indecipherable.

The cage wobbled. Viola's fingers cramped as she resisted the urge to scream.

A woman gasped: "How beautiful!"

Viola opened her eye and peered at the piazza below. The morning sun was still low on the horizon. It glinted off the water lapping the edges of the canal. Shimmering reflections danced on the bottom of the arched bridge.

The operator raised the control lever, slowing the chamber's descent. The clatter of the city and smell of brine infused the chilled air as it drifted through the chamber. A canal breeze lifted errant flurries of snow off the row of gondolas bobbing on the water.

Angry, overlapping voices drifted across the piazza, and were carried away over the canal. Handmade placards waved above a small crowd of men gathered at the edge of the piazza, confined behind a rope barricade. Two burly men in Company uniform stood on the near side.

The Ascension Chamber shuddered to a halt. The operator opened the chamber door and nodded in the direction of the Company men. They stepped forward, nudging the rope and stared down the crowd. The crowd settled and shifted restlessly.

"Welcome to Venezia, Ladies and Gentlemen." The operator directed Viola, Polly and their fellow passengers toward a steam-powered omnibus next to the tower. "The omnibus will take you to The Channel Airship Service's Offices to meet your loved ones."

Viola followed the other passengers toward the omnibus as the chamber ascended to retrieve the next group of travellers.

Polly eyed the group of men beyond the rope barricade. "Miss?" she whispered as she stepped closer to Viola.

"I'd heard the Gadgeteers were active in Europe," Viola replied, "but I never expected them to be so brazen, accosting innocent tourists."

"Gadgeteers?" asked Polly.

"It's the name given to the European industrialists lobbying to abolish the Mechanicals Permit restrictions. They want permission to sell their mechanicals freely in Britain."

Polly gasped. "Perhaps one day I could qualify for papers, and own a plectocycle of my own?" She clasped the carpetbag to her chest.

"Unfortunately, the Gadgeteers care little for those who can't afford them," replied Viola as she climbed up the omnibus steps and settled on one of the bench seats. It was narrow, but comfortable. Polly plopped down next to her.

"And I'm afraid Her Majesty is determined to keep the embargo, despite their protestations and the advice of Prince Albert," said Viola.

The luggage cart rumbled across the flagstones toward them; its contents were deposited in the luggage compartment with a thump.

Viola scanned the group of passengers: Next to Polly, a nurse fussed over an impeccably-dressed matron of a dizzy age. A young woman of means sat across from Viola, dressed fit for husband-hunting. Three young dandies sat behind them, puffing up their voluminous cravats ready for action. They laughed and winked at the *mademoiselle*. She blushed; her chaperone glared at the youths and frowned. A young girl climbed onto her seat to get a better view of the uneasy mob.

Viola raised an eyebrow. There was no sign of the top-hatted gentleman so fond of cigars.

A murmur rolled over the mob as the Ascension Chamber rattled back down toward the piazza. The mob quivered. The rope barricade slackened. The metal bollards clattered onto the cobblestones. The men surged toward the omnibus, brandishing their placards and shouting: *Libero commercio di aggeggio!*

The driver jumped onto the top step outside the omnibus and locked the door. The din grew louder as the Ascension Chamber climbed the tower. Two more Company men arrived and pushed back the mob.

"What are they shouting, mama?" The little girl shrank behind her mother.

"They want free trade for mechanicals, dear," replied the mother as she patted the girl on the back.

Polly grabbed the edge of the bench seat. "Are we safe, Miss?" Her voice quivered.

One of the dandies turned toward her and smiled. "They're a little rambunctious today, Signorina. I expect they are waiting for the new Attaché, but he won't show his face until his men arrive."

"Isn't that a little melodramatic?" asked Viola

The young man raised an eyebrow "Have you not heard?" he replied. "The last Attaché was found dead last month. In the canal."

Viola bit her lip. Perhaps his caution was not so melodramatic?

He leaned closer and whispered: "There were rumours the *Aggeggio Uomini* - the Gadgeteers as you call them - may have been involved."

Viola's stomach lurched at the revelation. She glanced back toward the Ascension Chamber; its doors remained closed. It seemed the Attaché had also heard the rumours.

She edged away from the window and peered at the mob as they jostled the omnibus. Most seemed to be workers and few business men - likely hired troublemakers. She placed her hand over the hidden pistol in her bustle pocket, relieved she had brought protection on the trip. Her fingers relaxed.

The Company men pushed their way to the omnibus and shoved the mob away from the vehicle. One of the agitators broke free, pressed against the window and stared at Viola.

"Free trade for mechanicals! Mechanical Rights for the working class." He thrust a calling card in her direction.

Viola flinched. Until now, the issue of mechanical access rights had been academic; this was too close for comfort. True, they did have a genuine grievance - mechanicals should benefit more than just the upper classes - but violence was not the way to convince the privileged to relinquish their exclusive access. It would only antagonise them more.

The omnibus driver kicked the protester's shoulder, shoved him away and climbed onto the front of the vehicle. The calling card fluttered onto the ground.

The door to the Ascension Chamber rattled open. The top-hatted gentleman stepped out, raised his cigar to his lips and eyed the mob.

"Sir, we must leave. Now." His scowling retainer stepped forward and ushered him to a waiting carriage on the opposite side of the piazza.

The protester jerked his head in the direction of the Ascension Chamber and grinned. *"Andiamo!"*

The mob turned and surged toward the Arrival Tower.

The omnibus swayed as the driver dropped into his seat and yanked on a lever. The engine chugged into life. The seat vibrated under Viola. The omnibus lurched forward. The young woman sighed with relief. The nurse grabbed the matron's arm and the child squealed.

"Finally," growled the dandy.

A dishevelled Company Man rushed up to the omnibus, jumped onto the step below the driver and muttered in his ear. The vehicle shuddered to a halt. The passengers gasped and grabbed their seats to keep their balance.

Steam rolled down the edges of the omnibus and clung to its windows. The seat steadied.

"What now?" grumbled the matron.

As the steam dissipated, Viola searched the piazza. The mob had pursued their quarry. What was the delay?

The man on the step unlatched the door and leaned into the omnibus.

"Our apologies for the inconvenience, ladies and gentlemen. There appears to be a problem with the—" He glanced up to the driver and nodded. "... engine. You will disembark here and be escorted to your hotel."

The passengers murmured, shifted in their seats and disembarked from the omnibus.

"What do we do now, Miss?"

Viola held her hand in front of Polly. "We wait."

"But the man said—"

"I know what he said." Viola watched as the porter removed the baggage from the vehicle, checked the tags and deposited each trunk next to a passenger. A Company Man stepped forward to attend each group, keeping one eye trained on the piazza. Viola frowned. "I want to know where the Gadgeteers have gone before I go anywhere."

"Perhaps we should have visited Paris instead," whispered Polly.

The Company Man turned to Viola. "You must leave now, Miss. Before—" He paused and straightened his shoulders.

"Before they return?"

The man nodded.

Polly gasped.

Viola dropped her hands into her lap. She was in a foreign country, unable to speak the language; her only acquaintances were friends of a friend whom she had yet to meet. There was no choice. She had to comply with his instructions.

"Everything will be fine, Polly," she said. "Do as the man says."

Viola's boots tapped on the flagstones as she stepped into the piazza. Her trunk thumped on the ground beside the omnibus track. She eyed a piece of paper near the metal rail. She picked it up. The edge of a muddy footprint obscured the lettering:

... Mechanicals
Gadgets for the People...

She flipped over the card:

REPEAL
Britain's Mechanical
Ownership Permits

It was a noble sentiment, a concept she had discussed with Sir Archibald on more than one occasion. The proposal could benefit many in the Empire. Viola slipped the card into her purse. But not if the Queen had her way.

Footsteps echoed through the piazza. The Company Man jerked his head in the direction of the sound. A gentleman with snow white hair and long, well-kept beard trotted closer; his crisp, dark suit stood out in contrast. A woman in a plain navy skirt, men's shirt and tie strode up behind him. The Company Man greeted the pair and accompanied them back to the omnibus.

"Buongiorno!" The bearded gentleman spoke in an affected accent.

"Welcome to Venice," said the woman. "I'm Sylvia, and this is my husband, Professor Algernon Woolington." She shook Viola's hand. "May I call you Viola?"

Viola nodded.

"Archie said you were in need of adventure." She grinned. "I do hope Venice has not disappointed you so far."

"I—"

"I apologise for the uncouth ruffians, my dear," said Professor Woolington. "They're mostly all bluster."

"One does get used to them," said Sylvia.

The Professor inclined his head toward the Company Man and lowered his voice. "The tracks have been sabotaged again."

"Surely they realised the new Attaché wouldn't travel in the omnibus with the other passengers?" asked the Company Man.

The Professor shook his head. "These Venetians are cunning. They leave nothing to chance."

Sylvia nudged her husband and cleared her throat. "And this is your companion?" she asked Viola.

"Polly is my..." Viola paused, and nodded. "Yes," she said.

Polly smiled, straightened her shoulders and inclined her head in greeting.

"Our man, Sims, will arrive shortly, to take the luggage." The Professor dropped a few coins into the Company Man's hand. His fingers curled around the coins and he fetched the trunks.

"You are not going to the hotel." Sylvia took Viola's arm in hers and glanced in the direction of the Ascension Chamber. "You're staying with us."

Viola's gaze followed Sylvia's. "One of the passengers mentioned the previous Attaché had an accident," she said.

"Accident?" Sylvia leaned closer, her voice barely a whisper. "He was found face up in the lagoon, Viola. They say he jumped." She took a deep breath. "We knew him, of course, and if he was depressed, then

I—"

"Ah, Sims, about time you got here." The Professor's voice carried across the piazza.

Sims arrived with a mechanical cart in tow. He loaded the trunks onto the cart and winked at Polly. Polly's face reddened. She stepped away, and joined Viola and Sylvia.

Polly twisted a fold of skirt in her fingers. "I think I'll write to Constable Cooper tomorrow," she said. "He'll want to hear all about Venice."

Viola covered her mouth, trying to hide her smile. It seemed Polly could be in for an adventure of her own.

A frigid wind howled through the laneway. Viola brushed errant snowflakes from her shoulders and tucked her gloved hands into the fur-lined pockets of her visite. She followed the Professors away from the piazza, in the opposite direction the Gadgeteers had taken in pursuit of the Attaché.

Pastel-stuccoed dwellings and ornately carved palaces with arched windows and columned balconies rose up around them, huddled close to protect each other from the late afternoon chill. The rhythmic thud of the luggage cart's wheels over cobblestones followed them. Polly remained silent, avoiding Sims' playful glances.

Snatches of laughter caught on the wind. The murmur of a crowd grew louder as they walked on.

"It's just beyond the next square," said Sylvia.

Music swelled.

"No need to worry," said the Professor. "It's the early entertainment for tomorrow's Carnevale celebrations."

Viola's eye widened. An entertainment? She paused and peered into the nearby piazza. Clutches of onlookers stood scattered throughout the piazza.

The crowd hushed. A distant roar of wind rushed above them, followed by gasps and applause.

Polly gasped.

Strains of violin music resumed and echoed eerily between the buildings and along the lane.

"Can we see?" asked Viola.

"Of course," replied Sylvia. "Sims, you go ahead. We shan't be long."

Sims nodded and continued along the laneway.

Polly glanced at Sims. "I should go, Miss."

Viola raised an eyebrow.

Polly's gaze flicked away; her ears tinged red. "To ensure the unpacking is done correctly."

"Thank you, Polly." Viola smiled. Poor Polly. She was just trying to do her job. She waved Polly away. "I'm sure Sims will follow your instructions."

Polly straightened her skirt, bobbed and followed Sims.

Viola stepped into the piazza and joined the outskirts of the closest group, all staring intently at the spectacle at its centre. Another roar filled the air. The crowd flinched. Orange flame shot a few feet skyward. Heat rolled over Viola's cheeks. The faint smell of warm paraffin wafted above them.

The audience clapped. Coins clinked on the ground.

A gunshot cracked above their heads. Viola flinched. Her head snapped in the direction of the noise. The violin music screeched to a halt.

The crowd murmured and shifted uneasily. Onlookers peeled away from the edges of the gathering and drifted toward the growing crowd on the other side of the piazza. Viola followed, joining the crowd coalescing around the new attraction.

"And now for a feat of courage few will attempt, and even fewer will survive." The voice was crisp, the English perfect.

A hush fell over the crowd.

The Professor squeezed his way to the front of the gathering. Sylvia grabbed Viola's hand and pulled her through the crowd after him. The assistant circled the edge of the crowd, brandishing a firearm, and eyed them studiously. "The Immortal Geovani will catch the bullet, fired from this very pistol, in his teeth," he said.

The audience gasped. The assistant's footsteps resounded ominously in the silence of the piazza, as he paced the edge of the crowd.

The Immortal Geovani bowed low. He was dressed plainly, no fancy cape or shiny top hat to conceal any sleight of hand.

Catch a bullet? Viola's heart raced. A man's jaw could not withstand the force of a fired bullet. It had to be a clever, if courageous, trick. She licked her lips. But how would he do it? Now that was a mystery worth investigating, one worthy of her detectiving skills.

The assistant handed Geovani the pistol.

"I require a volunteer." His voice carried across the piazza. "Preferably someone with good aim." He smiled.

Weak laughter spread through the crowd. The Professor chuckled.

"You, sir?" Geovani pointed to an elderly gentleman standing next to Viola. "Surely you have seen service?"

The gentleman nodded.

"You are experienced with a pistol?"

The gentleman nodded again.

"Eccellente." Geovani grinned and handed him the pistol. "Please check it is to your satisfaction and confirm it's not modified in any way."

The gentleman examined the firearm, nodded and returned it to Geovani.

"Bene." Geovani dropped a bullet in the gentleman's hand. "Make

your mark on the bullet, please, sir."

The man scratched the end of the bullet and handed it back. Geovani loaded it into the pistol and placed it in the gentleman's hand. He spread his arms and turned to address the crowd.

"Let it be known that I, The Immortal Geovani, declare this gentleman shall not be held responsible if I should fail." He stepped several feet back from the crowd, took a deep breath and nodded to his assistant.

The gentleman stared at the pistol in his hand.

"Are you ready, sir?" asked Geovani.

The gentleman's companions stepped back. Deep creases lined their foreheads. Viola held her ground, and peered at the pistol in his hand. Was it a fake? She squinted. It looked real enough.

Sylvia fussed beside Viola, tugging at her arm for her to step away. "It's not safe."

Viola waved Sylvia's hand away. She needed to concentrate. If only she could examine the pistol more closely. Perhaps she could solve the mechanics of the deception? Her heart skipped.

The assistant patrolled the edge of the crowd once more, his attention lingering on each individual as he passed. Viola tracked his gaze over the crowd - a mix of tradesmen, gentry and travellers. Wrinkles clawed the edge of his eyes. He was worried; the bullet catch was a dangerous performance, normally executed in the controlled environment of a hall or stage. People had died attempting it. Viola's heart shuddered. How could he control a random crowd, out in the open? Performing it here was folly. This man must either be fearless, or reckless. Or both.

The gentleman raised the pistol. His hand trembled. Viola heard his ragged breath. Wisps of vapour emanated from his mouth. Was he complicit in the illusion? If so, he was a good actor. Pinpoints of moisture beaded on his forehead. His finger twitched. Viola held her breath.

He straightened his arm, mirroring The Immortal Geovani's stance.

"Shoot!" The voice came from amongst the onlookers.

Viola winced. A murmur ran through the crowd. The assistant clenched his hand. He scanned the crowd, and lowered his stance, ready to pounce at any sign of danger.

The gentleman raised the pistol and stared down the barrel. Viola followed his line of gaze directly to the performer's head. She scrutinised his movements closely for any slip in the routine.

The Immortal Geovani raised his chin, looked the gentleman in the eye and nodded slowly. The murmurs became more insistent. The crowd's thirst for blood was whetted.

Worry lines on the gentleman's brow faded. His mouth hardened. Breath hissed as it escaped. The pistol trigger clicked. Its hammer slammed home. A crack rang in Viola's ear.

She flinched; pinpoints of heat pricked her cheek.

Geovani didn't blink. There was nothing: no movement, no sound. No reaction at all. Had the bullet missed? Without warning, he bellowed and doubled over.

A woman shrieked. Another fainted. Sylvia tensed. The Professor rushed forward. Viola stood her ground. The assistant held up his hand silencing the crowd and staying their approach. The crowd froze.

Sylvia's arm wrapped around Viola's shoulder. "Are you hurt?" She urged Viola away from the commotion. "You were standing too close."

"I am fine," replied Viola as she brushed her cheek.

Geovani coughed, slowly straightened and raised his hand to his mouth. He parted his lips. Metal glinted between his teeth. He grinned, letting the bullet fall into his hand.

Viola's heart skipped. Astounding! And impossible. She recounted the events in her mind and frowned. She'd seen the bullet go into the chamber, seen the muzzle flash. She turned her attention to the wide-eyed gentleman, his mouth gaping, like a suffocating fish gasping for air. The pistol hung loosely on his finger.

"Behold, The Immortal Geovani." The assistant swept his arm

theatrically in the direction of the performer.

Geovani bowed low, his hand almost scraping the flagstones. The audience cheered and clapped. The assistant removed his bowler, rolled it down his arm and presented it to the onlookers. Coins rained into the hat.

Soft snow fell on Viola's face and caught on her eyelashes. She dusted them off her bodice, not taking her eye off the smoking pistol. The gentleman *had* shot it... But how did...?

"Thank you, sir." Geovani plucked the pistol from the gentleman's hand and winked at Viola.

She raised an eyebrow.

Sylvia's arm tightened. "We'd better get you home," she said. "You must be tired after all this excitement, and after such a long journey." She glanced over the crowd.

"Yes, you must rest up for Carnevale tomorrow," said the Professor. "We've been invited to a party."

Their voices droned, barely audible above the ringing in Viola's ears. Her attention lingered on The Immortal Geovani. *How did he do it?* Her mind churned and twisted with possibilities. Viola straightened her shoulders and thrust her hands back into her *visite* pockets. She had some experimenting to do.

The last vestiges of daylight rimmed the rooftops, cloaking the canal in deep shadow. The morning snow and frigid sea winds had sealed the water's surface. Viola tugged at her cloak, glad to be out of the wind and in the protection of the ebony gondola's covered *felze*.

The gondola sliced through the water - a sliver of coal floating along the canal. She had already grown used to the constant lapping of the canals; the near silence of the frosted water was discombobulating.

The thin shell of ice tinked as it cracked under the bow. Viola sucked in the chill air and concentrated on the gondolier's song - a sad tune, something about *amoré* and Venezia.

The gondolier twisted the top of his articulated oar. It whirred. Its lower half clinked as it lifted from the water; its paddle flipped and stabbed at the frozen crust and propelled the gondola forward.

Viola marvelled at the contraption. How much easier life was with accessible mechanicals for all.

Viola pulled back the *felze's* curtain. The sofa creaked beneath her as she shifted to view the water. The prow lantern cast pools of light onto the canal. The ice was smooth and unblemished save for the scar left in their wake. A gust of wind cut across the surface, lifting flurries of snow and sealing the water's wound behind them.

Her gold mask hugged her face, like delicate metallic lace, creating a cold rim around her eyes and cheeks. She tugged the hood of her thick velvet cloak forward, to protect herself from the chill, and glanced at her companions. Painted leather masks obscured the Woolingtons' faces. Only a shock of white hair and a short, fiery-red mane betrayed them. Viola cupped her hands and directed her warm breath onto her mask and silently commended Sylvia's choice of costume, and practicality of fashion, once again.

The gondola tapped the landing and slipped into place beside a row of boats, which had already deposited their passengers. Their gondola nudged the edge as the Professor and Sylvia disembarked. Viola's cloak snagged on the prow. She shifted to keep her balance, as she tugged it free.

The gondolas clunked and rattled as they came and went. Waves of revellers continued to arrive, jostling each other as the crowd swelled. Viola eyed the swarming crowd of clowns, courtiers and masked villains. She wrapped her cloak snug around her torso and stepped gingerly onto the cobblestones.

"Are the stories true about Carnevale?" she asked,

"Anything goes, my dear. The only rule is: don't do anything you'll regret." The Professor grinned. "... and don't get caught by the Guardia."

Sylvia chuckled and pressed a few coins into the gondolier's open palm. "We'll be returning at midnight, Marco," she said.

Marco nodded. *"Sì, signora."* The gondola peeled away from the canal edge and slipped into the dark.

A second wave of gondolas arrived, ferrying more revellers in colourful and ever-more fanciful costumes.

The Professor slipped his arm around Sylvia's elbow and grinned. "Shall we, ladies?"

Viola turned to follow. The new arrivals streamed off their transports and flooded the street, separating her from the Professors. Viola clenched her cloak tighter, stretched up on tiptoe and searched the sea of feathered *capelli* and decorated hats. Sylvia's voice wafted over their heads. She waved her hand in Viola's direction and pressed forward, trying to push against the retreating tide.

"We'll meet you at the fountain in half an hour," she yelled above the chatter. "You—" Sylvia's mouth moved slowly, her words drowned out as they were carried along with the crowd.

Viola drifted, washed along by the crowd, toward a nearby bridge. A masked woman, in a red and green Harlequin costume, hovered fleetingly before her, twirled and floated away with the crowd.

Somewhere a flute played. Soft, lulling notes flitted through the air, winding through an unlit alley behind Viola. She turned and stared into the darkness. It *felt* familiar...

New arrivals glided past her, a blur of masks, colour and sparkle. Their words slurred. Laughter turned into snickers.

The beguiling notes wove their way around her and pushed the crowd, and the Harlequin, further along the path. Silhouettes peeled into the darkness. The music stopped.

A sudden jolt jerked Viola's shoulder. A giggling couple scampered away from the alley, in the direction the crowd had gone.

Viola shook her head. Perhaps she'd had too much wine at dinner? She blinked. Her vision cleared and focused on the retreating lovers. She followed them along the street. The sound of laughter grew louder as they approached a private residence.

Muscular lion statues of Istrian stone guarded either side of the arched entrance. Playful tunes enticed Viola closer. The smell of perfume, wine and sweat engulfed her, and dragged her toward the festivities. She paused and scanned the crowd as it swirled around the courtyard. A flash of red twirled near the fountain at its centre.

"Sylvia?" Viola could barely hear her own voice above the chattering din. She searched the crowd. Sylvia was gone.

Viola waded into the mass of shifting colour and squeals of glee, and made her way toward the fountain. A familiar scent filled her nostrils. A flutter of red and green shimmered in the corner of her eye. She turned. The female Harlequin stood motionless, just beyond arm's reach, and stared directly at her. Her lip curled. A shiver ran down Viola's spine. There was something. Those eyes...

Viola stepped closer. The green and red feathers, curving around the wide brim of the Harlequin hat, quivered. The woman's eyes widened. She twitched, tugged on her bodice and darted back into the crowd.

Those eyes; they reminded her of...

"Anne?" The name caught in Viola's throat. Her lungs convulsed. She gasped for air. Her head spun.

The muffled music continued as the crowd danced around her. Her heart thumped. She shook her head. She was imagining things. Yes, that was it. She'd heard dirigible travel didn't agree with some. Perhaps she had a touch of altitude sickness? She took a deep breath, to regain her balance.

A footman dressed in red and gold livery stepped forward, bowed and offered her a tray of drinks in sparkling, cone-shaped glasses of the palest blue. Viola took a glass. She could do with a drink to settle her nerves. She took a sip. Bubbles tickled her nose. Her heartbeat slowed.

She searched the courtyard, ignoring the powdered wigs and ornate masks. Green and red feathers were her quarry. The Harlequin hat bobbed amongst the crowd. It turned, hovered, and floated to the other side of the courtyard where a small gate led out into a laneway.

A hoard of boisterous merrymakers in French Aristocrat costumes surged forward, enveloping her and cutting off her path. A cloud of perfumed powder descended around them. Viola stifled a cough and tried to extricate herself from the group.

"To our host!" The cry reverberated around the courtyard. Precariously raised glasses jiggled with their cackling laughter.

"*Scusa.*" Viola dodged a drizzle of champagne, slipped past a pirouetting signorina in a lustrous gown Anglaise, edged through the revellers past the fountain and continued in pursuit of the Harlequin. The crowd folded in behind her, concealing any hint of her travail.

Viola pushed open the gate and entered an unlit lane. Footfalls faded into the distance, moving away from the canal. She stretched out and ran her gloved hand along the wall to guide her, and tracked the sound through the darkness into an adjoining street.

Street lamps lit a small piazza and reflected off the polished white theatre hall on the opposite side. Faint knocks and banging sounds issued from the alley next to the building. Torn posters lined the brick walls near the lane entrance near where she stood. They announced the new wonder of the age, a Master of Magic and Illusion. The mustachioed face of the magician stared back at her. Beside him was a female assistant in a sumptuous costume with an elaborate coiffure of braided blonde hair and ostrich feathers.

A ladder clattered on the nearby wall. A man balanced on it, scraped up the edge of a poster, tore it from the wall and climbed down again.

Paper remnants fluttered to the ground near Viola's feet. She examined them in the lamplight.

Viola gasped and snatched up the poster fragment. Those eyes... It was an exact likeness of Anne. Several years older than Viola remembered, but it was definitely her sister. Viola's heart seized in her chest, as if hit by a train.

"Anne?" Viola scanned the piazza. There was no sign of the Harlequin. She stepped into the light as the man climbed back up the ladder. *"Scusa?"* she asked.

The man slapped a new poster onto the wall.

"Lo spettacolo è terminato." His brush slid over the paper with a squelch.

"Finished?" Viola frowned. "Sorry, I don't—" She shook her head. *"Non capisco."*

The man shrugged his shoulders and continued with his work.

Viola clutched the poster and drifted toward the noises in the alley beside the theatre hall. She peered down the lane. Pools of light bobbed in the distance.

Viola clung to the poster remnant and trudged along the alley. She had to find out if the Harlequin was Anne.

Voices filled the alley. The strong smell of tobacco assaulted her nostrils. Lamp light outlined stacked crates and boxes piled up against the building. Workmen busied themselves moving crates onto trolleys. A bearded man climbed onto a crate on the trolley and tightened a rope. A cracking sound ricocheted off the building. He tumbled off the crate.

"Merda!" He snatched off his cap and slapped the head of the nearest worker. *"Idiota."* He rolled his shoulder. A red light glowed and faded near his mouth. Smoke circled his head as he turned to face Viola.

Viola paused. "Did a woman come this way?" she asked hesitantly. "She was wearing a costume."

"Che cosa?" The man jumped off the crate.

"I'm looking for a woman in a Harlequin costume..." She cleared her throat. *"Una donna?..."* Viola circled her fingers around her eyes. "In a mask...?"

The worker replaced his cap and brushed his hands on his trousers. "I am sorry." His English was stilted. *"Lo spettacolo* - the show, she is finished."

"Yes, but there was a woman. I need to know where—"

The man pulled the cigarello from his mouth. *"Andato."* He pointed further into the alley, toward the canal. "All gone."

Her heart twisted. Had she found Anne, only to lose her again? Viola struggled to slow her breathing. "Do you know where they went?"

"Andranno a Parigi," he replied.

Viola shook her head. "I don't understand."

He thrust his cigar in the direction of a crate next to her. "Paris."

Viola peered at the address label:

Ludovic, The Illusioneer Extraordinaire
Les Folies-Bergére
32 Rue Richer
9th Arrondissement, Paris

"Paris?" Viola's heart fluttered. The Woolingtons were taking her to Paris next week. Perhaps she could convince them to take the journey earlier? She smiled, opened her purse and dropped a few coins into his hand.

He grinned, tipped his cap and pocketed them before returning to work.

Viola turned and strode back toward the piazza. Footsteps tapped toward her. Two figures approached, silhouetted in the lamplight from the piazza. Viola slowed. Her heart thumped. She was alone in a foreign city...

"Viola?" It was Sylvia.

Viola's muscles relaxed.

"Whatever are you doing down here?" she asked. There was a hint of concern in her voice.

Sylvia skipped closer and wrapped her arm around Viola's shoulder. She sniffed and wrinkled her nose. "Champagne?" She raised an eyebrow. "Dare I ask?"

Viola shook her head. "Clumsy French aristos." She waved her hand dismissively. "It was too crowded in there," she said. "I had to get some fresh air."

The Professor caught up with them and stared into the alley. "Are you all right, Doctor Stewart?" he asked.

"I am perfectly fine." Viola smiled and dusted off her skirts.

He eyed the workmen through slitted lids, nodded and led her back to the piazza.

Viola tucked the poster into her skirt pocket. She had to leave for Paris and find *Ludovic, The Illusioneer Extraordinaire* as soon as possible, if she was to have any chance to discover if the Harlequin was indeed Anne.

"Sylvia, would you mind if we left earlier for Paris?" she asked.

The Professor eyed Viola. "We can't tempt you with a tour of the Doge's Palace tomorrow?" he asked.

Viola shook her head. "There's nothing left for me here," she replied.

"Then Paris it is," he said. "It will be the train, I fear. Can't get airship passage at such short notice."

The morning sun glinted off the brass window fixtures. Shadows swept across the blue upholstered seats of the first-class train compartment. The carriage clunked and shuddered as it turned eastward. Viola gripped the handle of her teacup. The liquid jiggled precariously close to the rim.

The Professors seemed oblivious to the disturbance; Sylvia glanced out the sash window and peered at the buildings as they passed.

"We're almost there," she said.

Viola smiled and sipped the last of her tea - a delicious blend of Assam and Darjeeling.

Professor Woolington turned the page of his newspaper and frowned. "It seems another attaché has disappeared," he said. "They really should employ more reliable public servants."

Viola placed her cup and saucer on the tray.

Sylvia checked the pendant watch on her neck chain and eyed the remnants of morning tea on the tea tray. "Better eat your cake, Algernon. The tray will have to be returned before we reach the station."

The top of the Professor's newspaper flopped forward, revealing the lines in his forehead.

Sylvia patted her husband on the knee. "If you don't eat it, then I shall," Sylvia taunted.

He folded up the newspaper and reached for the last piece of cake. Sylvia pushed his plate away from the side of the tray and pressed a button on the side of the table between the seats. Gears clicked inside. The crockery clinked quietly as the tray descended into the table and the top slid closed.

Viola could hear a faint rumble as it was carried away on an unseen conveyor system. Her eyes widened. There were so many fascinating mechanical aids in Europe. Her heart skipped. If only mechanicals were allowed freely in Britain. How useful they could be!

Sylvia raised an eyebrow. "You don't have a Mechanical Butler System in London?"

Viola shook her head. "They don't have a lot of things in London."

"I forgot," Sylvia tsked. "We've been abroad so long."

"Perhaps the Gadgeteers have a point?" said the Professor.

The Professor harrumphed. "But their methods...?" He slapped the folded newspaper on his leg. "And their behaviour!" He examined the piece of cake in his fingers with scientific precision. "If they didn't act like anarchists, then perhaps the Queen would consider their argument?"

Viola cleared her throat. "I should like to take in a show while in Paris," she said. "I hear there's a Magic Review at *Les Folies-Bergére*."

"Oh, what a jolly good idea," said Sylvia.

The Professor smiled. "Sir Archibald said you love a good puzzle."

"The Carnevale performers were most intriguing, weren't they," said Sylvia.

"Or are you *pursuing further enquiries*?" The Professor's lip flickered in a brief smile, as he popped the last piece of cake in his mouth, picked up the newspaper and continued reading.

Viola shrugged, hoping to deflect the Professor's comment. Though Sir Archibald had vouched for the Woolingtons, she barely knew them. She wasn't going to confide in relative strangers about family matters, at least not until all was settled.

"Is *Les Folies-Bergére* far from where we're staying?" she asked Sylvia.

Sylvia shook her head. "A short carriage ride only. I'll have Sims fetch tickets this afternoon."

The compartment door slid open.

"Good morning." Polly entered the compartment, her carpetbag in one hand. A wandering hat feather fell across her vision. She batted it away, defiantly.

"Good morning, Polly," said Sylvia. "I'm afraid you've just missed morning tea."

Polly slipped the carpetbag onto the floor between the seat and the table, sat on the seat next to Viola and tugged at the feather.

"Did you manage to post your letter to your Constable Cooper, in Lyon?" asked Viola.

Polly shook her head. "No." Her shoulders slumped. "I couldn't find any sealing wax in the luggage, Miss."

"That's strange." Sylvia turned to Polly. "I asked Sims to pack a new box yesterday. I have a mountain of correspondence to finish before the weekend."

Viola bit her lip and busied herself reading the personal advertisements on the back of the newspaper.

Professor Woolington peeked over the over the top of the paper, directly at Viola. Her cheeks burned. She redirected her attention to her skirts and flicked an unseen, stray crumb from the pleated trim.

Sunlight dimmed as the train turned westward. The carriage rattled as the train crossed several more tracks. A quiet knock tapped on the compartment door. An attendant leaned into the compartment.

"We arrive at Gare de Lyon in ten minutes," he said. "Will you require assistance?"

"No, thank you," replied the Professor. "Our man, Sims, will do it."

The attendant tipped his blue and black *kepi*. "Then, on behalf of Paris-Lyon-Mediterranean, I wish you an enjoyable stay in Paris."

Viola stepped onto the platform as another train chugged away from the other side of the station. Steam and smoke belched into the air, blanketing the skylights of the peaked ceiling and blocking the light filtering through the sooty glass. Strands of vapour drifted down and curled above her head. The smell of coal dust and smoke settled around her.

Viola wrinkled her nose, stifled a cough and scanned the station.

She'd expected more splendour in one of the major thoroughfares of Europe.

Overlapping voices grew louder as more passengers swarmed off the train and filled the platform. Smudges of colour and floating feathered hats criss-crossed the drab platform, as the new arrivals made their way to the exit.

Sylvia stepped onto the platform beside her. Polly and Professor Woolington joined them.

"It isn't much to look at, is it?" whispered Sylvia.

Viola nodded. The *Gare de Lyon* was like the dowdy rich aunt whom everyone courts and flatters but no one would own in public.

"They are always arguing over whether to spend money on improvements," said the Professor.

A loud clunk rolled across the station. Vents opened just below the skylights. The air seemed to shudder. Air currents caught the wisps of smoke and syphoned them out of the station.

"At least they've finally installed some mechanicals to clear this blasted coal smoke," he said.

They made their way toward the ornate, wrought iron double gates at the end of the building. Gigantic clocks crowned the central pillar. Posters lined the walls: bright green advertisements for Absinthe flanked colourful, risqué posters for the *Moulin Rouge*. Faded glimpses of the Eiffel Tower adorned dog-eared remnants of advertisements announcing last year's *Exposition Universelle*.

Viola sighed. They would have been new and colourful when Sir Archibald had attended the World Fair. Had the wonders of the age already become so common-place here, in Paris?

A trolley, overloaded with trunks and portmanteaus, rumbled along a narrow-gauge rail, from the luggage carriage along the platform. Sims dodged through the crowds, following the trolley toward the ticket gates.

The train track rumbled. A horn blared as a second train chugged into the station and halted at the far platform. The air shuddered again; the breeze strengthened. The crowd swelled and surged toward the gates, sweeping Viola and her companions away from their train.

A ticket collector stood at the base of the central pillar between the gates, beneath the clocks. He held out his hand and stared over the crowd with an unfixed gaze. Sylvia handed him two tickets. Viola delved into her bag, pulled out her ticket and handed it to the collector.

"Bienvenue à Paris." His voice was flat. He nodded and waved them through the gate.

The clocks' ticks were surprisingly loud. They whirred and clunked. A single gong filled the air. Viola glanced up. A quarter past the hour. She lifted her neck chain and adjusted her watch to local time. There was a lot of work to do.

The grand hall of *Les Folies-Bergére* shone with elaborate swathes of bright-coloured silk gowns, dazzling jewels and immaculately-pressed tailcoats. Viola's heart raced; Not because of the spectacular display of fashionable elite, nor the grandeur of the double staircase leading up to the mezzanine - where the *beau monde* looked down on Parisian society - nor the whimsy of the trapeze artist swinging above their heads. She was here for one thing only: would the Harlequin be on stage tonight? And was it truly Anne? Had she finally found her sister after all these years?

She took a deep breath, straightened her opera gloves and adjusted the buttons at her wrists. She must remain calm.

Professor Woolington skirted around the edge of the tables set near the bar and twisted past cliques of patrons, three *Pontalier* glasses with a green, almost iridescent, cloudy liquid in his hands.

Viola fidgeted with her purse.

He glanced at her hands and handed a glass to her, and another to Sylvia.

"You look like you need something to calm your nerves, Doctor Stewart. And when in Paris..." He grinned.

Viola eyed the pale liquid. It danced in the lamplight. Perhaps something to fortify her courage was permissible. Facing ghosts of the past was not an everyday occurrence.

"I can do this," Viola whispered to herself.

"Of course, it is only a small drink," said Sylvia. "And it's not at all unpleasant." she quaffed her drink and licked her lips.

Viola smiled. She had not meant the drink; she'd survived stronger biologics. She took a deep breath. But could she face the truth... of Anne?

She raised the chilled glass to her lips. A dry, pungent aroma caressed her olfactory senses. She closed her eyes and sipped. The taste was unexpected: crisp and sweet, reminding her of childhood family dinners, with roast fennel. She smiled; Anne disliked fennel intensely.

Viola swallowed. Her muscles relaxed. She knew it wasn't the drink; there'd been scarcely time for it to leave her tongue. No, she had decided. She had to know the truth - damned or not. She eyed the untouched glass of Absinthe in the Professor's hand. He relinquished the glass and raised his eyebrow.

"Time to go," whispered the Professor.

She drained his glass. The aftertaste was unexpected - like an unsweetened lemon: bitter yet not disagreeable. She placed the glasses on the nearest table and followed Sylvia and Professor Woolington toward the left staircase.

Sylvia's silk velvet gown shimmered in the light - the colour of Absinthe, flowing like pale green liquid as she ascended the stairs. Gold and silver embroidered vines and flowers tumbled from the shoulders onto the bodice, swirled down the skirt and cascaded onto the train.

The Professor's suit was exquisitely tailored, a match in both simplicity and elegance. The Venetians must pay their scientists well. His hand slipped from Sylvia's waist and rested on her hip, unafraid to show affection in public. When in Paris...

Viola blushed and tried to concentrate on the task at hand.

Sylvia giggled. Viola's gaze wandered back to the couple. The Professor took his wife's hand and squeezed it gently, as they reached the top stair. He turned to Viola and smiled.

Viola's heart raced. For a moment she saw Henry's face, could feel his breath on her neck. Her heart ached, as if it had been ripped from her chest. There was a hole where Henry should be. She twisted the ring on her left hand. She longed for him to be here, beside her, holding her hand as she neared the end of her quest. More than anything, she wanted to return to London, to her Henry.

The doors to the balcony opened. Haunting music drifted along the mezzanine, beckoning the patrons to their seats. It had started: the beginning of the end of her quest.

Viola took a deep breath and stepped into the hall.

Viola edged along the front row of the balcony seats.

"I do apologise." Sylvia sat down beside her and fetched her opera spectacles from her purse. "These were the only seats available."

Viola peered over the balcony rail. The stage was scarcely a hundred yards from them.

"You won't need those," said Professor Woolington. "It's a perfectly good view."

"Oh, good." She stuffed the spectacles back into her purse and settled into her seat. "It seems this Illusioneer's reputation preceded him. This is a special performance for the *Académie des sciences* and visiting dignitaries from America."

The Professor leaned toward Viola. "Fortunately, I have a friend at the *École Normale Supérieure*, who is a member," he whispered.

"Algernon has friends *everywhere*," said Sylvia.

"How fortunate," said Viola.

She smiled and surveyed the theatre: it was cloaked in crimson - crimson-upholstered seats, crimson carpet and crimson fabric-lined walls. Luxurious curtains of blood-red velvet lined the stage. Deep swathes of velvet draped across the top of the heavy front curtain. Cream-coloured columns framed the stage.

The front curtain twitched and eased open. A lone, octagonal table of polished mahogany stood in the centre of the stage, illuminated by a single, dim light.

A murmur rolled over the auditorium. The audience stirred in their seats and turned their attention to the stage. Footsteps clicked across the wooden floor, echoing above their heads. The audience hushed.

One by one, the limelights erupted into life, and converged on the table.

A man clad in a fitted tailcoat, red waistcoat and expensive top hat, walked into the light and stood by the table. Without a word, he bowed and pulled a large handkerchief from his inside coat pocket, presented it to the assembly and draped it over the table. He tugged at his sleeve cuffs, pinched the centre of the handkerchief theatrically in his fingers and paused.

"Science suggests all matter is made from the same particles: *the theory of the universe*." His voice was clipped, with a hint of accent. "But what if this matter could be controlled?"

The Illusioneer eyed the audience and grinned. Viola shifted in her seat.

"What if one held the power to create...?" He whipped the cloth away from the table, with a flourish of his wrist, to reveal a pair of doves in an octagonal birdcage about a foot high.

Viola eyed the cage, as applause rained around her. It was a simple trick; mirrors, perhaps?

He slipped a hand into the cage, removed one of the birds and presented it to the audience.

"Or the power to destroy." He dropped the handkerchief and let it settle over the cage. He turned his attention to the dove in his left hand and rubbed his cheek against its beak, as he raised his right hand and slammed it onto the concealed cage, collapsing it onto the table with a loud, resounding thud.

A woman screamed in the front row.

Viola sucked in her breath. It was a trick; it had to be. He wouldn't dare draw blood in such a gathering.

Viola held her breath and peered at the table as he lifted the cloth into the air. No bird, no cage. Nothing. The table was unblemished.

The Illusioneer stepped back and cupped the remaining dove in both hands. "True magicians do not cloak their genius." He thrust the bird into the air.

Viola examined each flurry of his fingers, each twitch of his hand. She could decipher the trick. Given time.

Flame roared into the air and the bird was gone.

Viola flinched, not taking her gaze from The Illusioneer. He was ingenious - and brazen - not using an assistant to deflect attention from each trick. Viola's heart sank. Perhaps she had been mistaken, and chasing the poster advertisement was a fool's errand.

"For my next illusion, I shall need an assistant."

Viola's heart skipped. She leaned forward and scanned the crowd. Had she been too hasty?

The Illusioneer stepped up to the edge of the stage. "I require a volunteer."

Viola shrank back into her seat. No good ever came of volunteering. She did not wish to be a reluctant substitute assistant. Again.

"You, sir?"

Not Anne. Was she wasting her time? Had she traced the wrong performer? Viola took a deep breath and leaned forward in her seat. A middle-aged man, in a full beard and moustache, a well-tailored suit and cravat rose from his seat in the front row.

"That's Monsieur Gustave Eiffel," whispered Sylvia.

"The engineer?" asked Viola.

Sylvia nodded.

"He's braver than I thought," said the Professor.

M. Eiffel smiled and ascended to the stage.

The Illusioneer waved his hand in the direction of the stage wings. The side curtain lifted to reveal a cogged contraption, with a lever and large crank wheel, resembling a pulley system. A chain ran from the middle of the cog-assembly up to the ceiling. The Illusioneer cranked the wheel forward. Gears clunked, chains rattled. Puffs of steam hissed from the contraption's workings. A man-sized, rectagonal cage settled on the stage with a clunk.

"Do you like to travel?" asked The Illusioneer.

"*Oui.*" M. Eiffel glanced at the ceiling and shifted uncomfortably. "As long as I can keep my feet on the ground."

The Illusioneer grinned and gesticulated theatrically with his hand. An eye mask appeared between his fingers. He offered it to M. Eiffel.

M. Eiffel's fingers stiffened, almost imperceptibly. Viola's hands clenched in sympathy. He wouldn't want to show fear in front of Paris' scientific elite.

The Illusioneer strode around the cage, unlatched its door and ushered M. Eiffel toward the cage. He hesitated.

"I assure you, Monsieur, the transportation cage is completely safe."

M. Eiffel nodded, stepped into the cage and clasped his hands behind his back. The Illusioneer latched the door and clicked a padlock in place. The keys jangled on his belt as he returned to the contraption and pulled on the lever.

A flash of light fluttered in the rafters. A shimmering cloth of gold descended and enveloped the cage, reminiscent of the original disappearing birdcage trick. Chairs creaked behind Viola as the audience squirmed in their seats.

Sylvia gasped. "Surely, he wouldn't!" She clasped her husband's arm.

The Professor leaned forward, resting his arms on the balcony rail. "This could be interesting," he whispered.

"Shh." Sylvia kicked him lightly on the leg.

Viola joined him and rested her arms on the rail.

The Illusioneer strode around the covered cage and lifted his arms as if revering his creation, then returned to the pulley contraption and pushed the lever. The gold cloth shivered and slowly lifted from the cage.

The crowd gasped. The limelights on the empty cage dimmed, others illuminated the Illusioneer.

Viola smiled. It was an impressive optical illusion. She craned her neck, trying to glimpse the side of the cage for any clue of its execution. He was clever, ensuring the audience could not see any crucial elements of the deception.

The Illusioneer bowed low, lapping up the applause. "While Monsieur is travelling, I shall require another—"

A piercing scream cut through the air. "She's gone!"

Heads spun to face the distraught woman. Was she part of the act? Viola leaned over the balcony railing. The woman stared, open mouthed, at the vacant seat beside her. Nearby spectators fussed over her. Viola turned her attention back to the Illusioneer. He was calm. Not a hint of surprise at all. Viola raised an eyebrow. *Curious.*

The woman glanced up at the stage and exclaimed. Her eyes widened as she slowly pointed at the cage.

Was this it? A misdirection, a prelude to the introduction of his assistant?

The lights illuminated the cage. A cloaked figure stepped out of the cage, face hidden, and walked forward. Viola noticed a faint limp. The Harlequin?

Viola edged forward on her seat and gripped the balcony rail. She held her breath. Anne!

A delicate hand slipped out from under the folds of the cape and unhooked its clasp. The cloak fluttered to the ground. A woman stood, head down, in the light. Blonde curls tumbled forward to conceal her face. She was dressed in an elegant form-hugging gown. The skirt was ruched over one hip, exposing a stockinged calf, and draped low over the other leg.

Viola rose from her seat. The woman raised her face to the light and flicked her cascading curls back over her shoulder.

Viola gasped and froze, half-standing, unable to breathe.

"Ladies and gentlemen, my beautiful assistant, Amélie." announced the Illusioneer.

"No," whispered Viola. It was *Anne*. Even after ten years, she was certain. It *was* her.

Viola's hands gripped the balcony until her knuckles paled and her finger muscles spasmed. A sharp pain shot through her empty eye socket.

A gentle hand touched her arm.

"Are you all right, Viola?" asked Sylvia.

Viola waved her away. Her vision blurred. Both performers glided gracefully across the stage, like choreographed dancers, performing their routines of magic and illusion. Viola's gaze followed Anne as she assisted the Illusioneer. They seemed to float, their movements slow and deliberate. Could Anne see her in the balcony? Would she recognise her?

"What's wrong?" Sylvia's voice was muffled, her hand now heavy on Viola's arm.

Viola forced breath into her lungs and stretched her fingers slowly.

"Viola?" The words were but a whisper.

Viola nodded slowly, her attention not leaving Anne. She blinked again.

Anne smiled, curtsied and swept her arm in the direction of the Illusioneer. Her gaze ran across the lower auditorium. She rose, and redirected her attention to the balcony seats. She scanned the crowd, and paused - looking directly at Viola. Every muscle in Viola's body refused to move, like a rabbit mesmerised by coach lights.

Anne's eyes widened. Her mouth hardened. She turned awkwardly and glanced at the Illusioneer as he took another bow, revelling in the accolades. She regained her composure, curtsied ostentatiously, not taking her eyes off Viola.

Viola swallowed. Why was Anne not pleased to see her?

The Illusioneer took her hand. They bowed in unison.

"But, alas, dreams cannot last forever and we must return to reality. All must be as it was." He released Anne's hand.

Anne stepped back into the transportation cage. The door shut with a loud click behind her. The Illusioneer returned to the contraption and pulled the lever. The gold cloth floated down onto the cage.

"It is a simple thing to make matter appear, or disappear." He cranked the wheel. The chain rattled, tautened and winched into the air until it hovered just above head-level. The hem of the gold cloth shivered below the cage. He locked the wheel in place and paraded around and under the suspended cage. It jiggled and wobbled above his head.

"That is a simple conjuring trick," He returned to front centre stage, the suspended cage behind him in full view. "But what if that matter could be transformed? Alchemists have toiled for centuries to perfect matter transmutation."

The centre stage lights brightened. Glimmering reflections spilled across the stage.

"I, Ludovic, Illusioneer *Extraordinaire*, have discovered their secret."

The cage lurched, slipping down a few links on the chain.

The crowd gasped. The cogs whined and crunched. The wheel jolted and spun. The cage wobbled and dropped.

The Illusioneer lunged at the pulley contraption, grabbed the crank wheel and pushed his weight against it. Steam gushed and squealed from the contraption. The wheel ground as the cogs caught and held. The covered cage stopped with a jolt, still several feet from the stage floor.

The cloth danced violently. The patches of reflected light flitted across the ceiling and walls, and glared in Viola's eye. An eerie silence fell across the auditorium. The audience stood motionless and held a collective breath. A few men sprang from their seats and raced toward the stage.

A sickening crack rolled along the roof. The cage shuddered, thundered onto the stage and collapsed. The walls clanged to the floor.

A woman wailed, breaking the silence and heralding a flood of shouts and cries of dismay.

The cloth slumped down and clung to an upright form standing where the cage had been. The crowd hushed. The rallying men halted mid-step. They stared at the shrouded phantasm, glowing under the limelight like a gilded ghost.

The Illusioneer stepped forward and dragged the cloth away from the form to reveal M. Eiffel, eye mask still in place and hands behind his back as if he'd never left the stage. The crowd stared silently at him. Anne was nowhere to be seen.

Viola collapsed into her seat, forcing the breath from her lungs.

Sylvia sat down next to Viola. "It was all part of the performance?" she asked, a distinct hint of relief, and annoyance, in her voice.

"Welcome back, Monsieur," said The Illusioneer.

"But I never—" M. Eiffel removed the eye mask.

A single, slow clap reverberated in the stall below them. An audible

sigh of relief swept through the crowd. One by one, they joined in the acclaim until applause and cheering filled the room.

Viola stretched her fingers slowly. The look on Anne's face... It was a look of shock. And... anger? Why anger? And where had Anne been all these years?

The Professor snatched up his hat and slapped it on his head. "The cheek! It's enough to give one a seizure. I shall complain to the proprietors." He turned to Sylvia. "How are you, my dear?"

Sylvia nodded and waved her hand in dismissal.

"Doctor Stewart?" he asked.

Viola composed herself. She had to go. She had to find Anne. She couldn't lose her again. She sighed and fanned her face. "It is hot in here, isn't it?" she replied, feigning a swoon.

"Oh, dear Viola!" Sylvia placed the back of her hand on Viola's forehead. "You look pale."

Viola pulled herself to her feet. "I just need some air." She edged past the Professors and hastened along the aisle.

"Wait! Viola..." Sylvia's voice faded behind her, drowned out by the blood rushing through her ears.

The evening air was crisp. Viola pulled up her long opera gloves and hurried into the lane beside the *Folies-Bergére*, leaving the light of the street lamps behind her. Her head spun. Her cheeks burned. Every step reverberated in her head, competing with the pain in her eye. Viola leaned on the theatre wall to steady her balance and wiped her forehead.

A brisk wind ushered her further along the unlit lane. She followed the wall around the corner to the theatre's back door. A pool of warm gaslight, from the wall fixture above the door, bathed the steps.

A lone *fiacre* - much like a Hackney cab - waited. Its lamps burned, illuminating the alley beyond. Viola relaxed. Perhaps she wasn't too late.

The wind clawed at her bare arms and fidgeted with her silk skirts. Goosebumps ran up her arms and down her spine. She could not forget the look in her sister's eyes. It wasn't surprise, but resentment. Anne had *not* looked pleased to see her. Viola shivered. Not from cold, but... She had to find out the truth.

The stage door creaked open.

Viola ducked back around the corner of the building and peeked into the lane.

The Illusioneer stepped into the alley. A dark cloak hung from his shoulders. He pulled on his white dress gloves, paused and turned back to face the doorway.

"Do come, Amélie. We'll be late."

Anne stepped gingerly down the steps and glanced along the alley.

Viola shrank back into the shadows, thankful she had not been swayed by Sylvia's insistence on purchasing a pale blue outfit; her midnight-blue evening gown would not betray her.

Anne took the Illusioneer's offered hand and stepped into the cab.

Viola's fingers tingled. The edges of her vision blurred. She rubbed her eye and struggled to focus.

The Illusioneer leaned toward the driver. "*Six Boulevard des Capucine,*" he instructed. The cab rocked as he climbed in.

Viola's muscles relaxed. The edges of the cab softened. Light streaked along the alley. Viola closed her eye. It was not to be unexpected; alcohol did affect the lenticular muscles. The Absinthe must have been stronger than expected. She leaned heavily against the wall and took a deep breath to try to clear her vision.

A pale figure approached the cab. Who was it? Viola blinked. The figure remained foggy.

Botheration! Perhaps she should have reconsidered that second drink.

The Illusioneer leaned out of the carriage window. What were they saying? Viola stepped away from the wall and strained to hear. Their whispers caught in the wind and were whisked away.

She closed her eye. Botheration!

The pale form slapped the side of the cab. "Drive on."

It trundled away, toward the far end of the alley.

Viola's head spun. She fell back against the wall. The figure hesitated, for what seemed like an eternity. Viola held her breath. Finally, it turned and retreated through the stage door.

Viola sighed and cradled her throbbing head in her hands.

Footsteps echoed along the alley. Viola glanced back toward the main street. Two hazy shapes approached.

Viola's fingers fumbled for her bustle pocket - and her pistol - to find only the voluminous, smooth folds of her newly-purchased gown, tailored in the latest Parisian fashion.

"Botheration!" There had been no time to have the seamstress tailor the gown to her requirements. *And* she'd left her pistol in London. She sniffed. Damnation!

"Viola?" Sylvia moved into the edges of the lamplight. "Thank goodness. I thought we might find you here." Deep furrows lined her forehead. "You seem to have a predilection for dark alleys."

"You forgot your cloak." said the Professor.

Sylvia examined her. "You must be freezing."

Spots of rain caught on her lashes. Viola shook her head and rubbed her arms, as if chasing away a chill. The alcohol had been good for something, at least.

"We need to get you home," Sylvia started back down the lane. "I'll fetch a cab before you start chasing fairies."

The Professor wrapped Viola's cloak around her shoulders. "Perhaps a second glass was not your best decision?"

Viola raised an eyebrow. He was direct; she could see how he and Sir Archibald got along.

"Are you still pursuing enquiries?" A gentle smile flickered over his lips. "Or have you found a mystery to solve?" His voice was barely audible. "Sir Archibald is a loyal friend. If he trusts you, then so do I." He bowed his head in her direction. "If I can assist you in any way...?"

"The offer is appreciated, but unnecessary." Viola caught the edges of her cloak, pulled it snug around her body and eyed the Professor. How much did he know?

"As you wish." He reached into his pocket, removed a pistol and pressed it into her hand. "At least let me offer you some protection for next time you go sneaking off on an adventure."

Viola smiled. "I am very grateful, Professor."

"Please, call me Algernon."

Viola slipped the pistol under her cloak and pulled up the hood to ward off the rain. "Thank you, Algernon."

Fog camouflaged the grey sandstone apartments and shrouded the bare trees lining the boulevard. The only smudges of colour were plastered on the octagonal kiosk on the footpath beside her, and in curtains scattered throughout the building.

Crowds strolled along the boulevard and browsed the shops on the ground level. *Fiacre* cabs lined the street on the opposite side. Horses tails twitched in impatience. One splendid mare skittered, held tight by his driver.

Viola lifted her shawl over her head and wrapped it around her neck to keep out the chill, and stood behind the kiosk to watch the entrance. Could she be certain Anne was at home alone? And would she be welcome?

A man wearing an Inverness coat rushed from the building to the nearest cab. He lifted his face to the driver. It was the Illusioneer.

"*École Normale Supérieure*." His clipped accent was distinctive.

Viola's heart raced. Now was her chance. She waited until the cab turned down *Avenue de l'Opèra*, and pulled the edge of her shawl up to hide her face from the prying eyes of the apartment concierge.

She picked her way through puddles as she crossed the cobblestones and jumped over the rivulet of water filling the gutter. Water dripped from the edge of a café's canvas awning as it was caught in the wind. Viola slipped past into the apartment entrance and climbed the wide staircase to the second floor.

She scanned the doors. There was no convenient name to confirm the address. Viola took a deep breath and rang the bell of apartment number One.

Her heart sunk in her chest. What if Anne refused to see her? What if...?

Muffled footsteps approached the door.

What if she had the wrong address? Yet again, she was alone in an unfamiliar city. Viola patted the reassuring weight in her skirt pocket. At least she had the Professor's pistol for protection.

The door opened. A petite, raven-haired young woman looked her directly in the eye.

"Yes?" she said.

"Is A—?" What did the Illusioneer call her? Viola cleared her throat. "Is Madame Amélie at home to visitors?"

The maid held out a small silver plate for a calling card. Viola's heart raced. Did the maid know Anne was using an assumed name? If not, announcing herself as Anne's sister would be imprudent. No, she couldn't use her own card.

Viola waved away the tray with a theatrical flourish. "I have no need for such antiquated ceremony." She feigned an accent. "I am being sent to ask Madame Amélie and the *Extraordinaire* Ludovic if they would consider come to my country."

The maid sighed, tapped the tray against her leg and led Viola into the parlour

"Wait here." She turned on her heel, strode out and closed the door.

The parlour was spacious, with high, ornate ceilings, polished oak wood floors and exquisite furniture. A crackling fire warmed the room.

Muffled voices spoke outside the door. Silence. The door creaked open.

Anne walked into the room, her limp barely noticeable. "I don't know how I can help you."

Viola slowly unwound the scarf from her face.

Anne turned to face Viola. "My husband is—" She paused mid-sentence. Her eyes widened. She glanced outside the room and clicked the door shut behind her.

"You can't be here," whispered Anne. "Ludovic will be returning soon." She bit her lip.

Viola shook her head. "We have time. He caught a cab to *École Normale Supérieure.*"

Anne remained near the door. "I thought it was you." She crossed her arms. "But I wasn't certain." She drifted over to the French window.

"Is James not with you?" Anne twisted the wedding finger on her left hand.

"Jac—?" An unseen force punched Viola in the gut. "James Findlay?" The words were forced as she struggled to catch her breath.

Anne nodded.

Viola remembered Anne's parting letter. She had left him to Viola, not knowing the end of the story. Viola leaned on the back of a nearby chair and regained her composure. "I don't know where he is," she replied.

Anne's mouth opened. "But I—" She scoffed as she parted the

curtain a crack and peered out onto the street. "You and father didn't want me to see him. You wanted him for yourself."

"He wasn't the man we thought he was," said Viola. Jealousy? Viola bit her lip. That's why Anne wasn't pleased to see her? If only she'd realised the lucky escape she'd had!

Viola stepped forward. "You did well to leave. James proved..." She smiled awkwardly. "Unsuitable."

"Unsuitable? Just because he didn't have a title, and wasn't rich?" She strode toward Viola. "I loved him, Viola. But he only wanted you." Anne clenched her hand. "It was always you! Father's favourite, university, beaus."

"Anne," her voice was calm, "he lied to us all."

"No, *you're* lying!" Anne raised her hand and slapped Viola across the face.

Viola gasped and clasped her cheek. Her hand was cold on the hot skin. Her face stung.

"Anne." Viola's voice remained calm. "He's wanted by Scotland Yard."

Anne rubbed her hand in silence.

"For the murder of several women," Viola whispered.

The door handle rattled and turned. Anne wiped a tear from her eye. The maid entered the parlour and bobbed a curtsy. "*Tout va bien, madame?*" She eyed Viola.

"*Oui*, Marie." Anne turned back to the window. "Tea, I think?" She smiled. "And cake."

The tea set was of fine bone china. A delicate wreath of forget-me-nots encircled the rim. Anne's hand trembled as she placed a cup and saucer on the table near Viola. Only the best for her guests.

She glanced at the parlour door - safely locked and bolted. They were alone. She regarded Viola. As children, they had been inseparable, sharing their secrets from the world. She had the same auburn hair; she'd teased her sister about it when they were children. She glanced into Viola's green eye - like a cat's; always watching, waiting for her moment to pounce.

Anne sipped her tea, trying not to stare at Viola's eye patch. They were more alike than she realised. But could she still be trusted?

Viola removed her gloves, folded them and placed them on the chair beside her. An engagement ring glinted on her finger.

"Anyone I know?" asked Anne as she placed a strainer on Viola's cup and poured the tea.

"You met him in Edinburgh once. He was a friend of Donell's."

"Ah, yes, the English one? Henry... something?" Anne filled her own cup. "He always seemed sweet on you." She smiled. "He took his time."

Viola sipped her tea.

Anne followed the ritual: tea, cake and smiles. "And are you living in Paris, or just taking in the sites on a Grand Tour?" she asked.

"Visiting with friends," replied Viola.

Viola's cup clinked on the saucer. There was an awkward silence. Anne eyed the swirling liquid in her cup. There was so much to be said; so many years, so many regrets...

Viola leaned closer and spoke: "I searched for you, Anne."

A stray tea leaf circled Anne's cup. She sipped the hot liquid. The comforting warmth spread into her chest.

"For years." The rims of Viola's eyes reddened. "Where did you go?"

Anne pushed a cake crumb around the edge of her plate. "I ran away." The skin on her neck warmed. "To join the circus."

A smile flickered over Viola's lips. She raised her tea cup to her lips.

"Don't laugh, please." Anne's ears burned. "I wanted to embarrass

Father." She took a deep breath. "We used to fantasise about it as children, remember?"

"And you met your Ludovic there?"

"He was kind to me." Anne popped a piece of cake in her mouth. The sweet apple reminded her of happier times, when she was free to make her own decisions. How could she admit she'd made so many mistakes since then? "I owe him."

Viola's eyelids flickered. "But are you happy?"

Anne's heart raced. She didn't reply. She'd spent too many years being careful with her words. Too many years not questioning, wondering whom she could trust.

Viola placed a gentle hand on Anne's. Anne held her breath, slowly slipped her hand away from Viola's touch and placed them on her lap. She glanced at the door. Still closed. She ventured a shallow breath.

Viola's gaze followed Anne's to the door. "You don't have to stay. He doesn't own you." She wiped a tear from her cheek. "Come back and stay with me in London."

"I can't," said Anne.

"Poppycock. Henry will be so pleased to finally meet you." She sat on the edge of her seat. "You can't say here."

Anne longed to return home, but there were impediments. She lowered her eyes. "I can't return with this." She caught up the hem of her skirt and raised it above her knee to reveal a brass prosthetic leg. Gears whirred silently as she moved the foot. "I don't qualify for a permit; it would be confiscated and I'd be left to beg in the streets. But even here, mechanicals are not cheap."

"How did...?"

"An accident. I fell. Ludovic paid for it. I owe him." She let the skirt fall back to the floor. "Besides, who else will have me now?"

Viola scoffed.

"Please don't think ill of him, Viola. He's promised to help. He has a plan," said Anne. There was just one task to complete before she could remain safe in Britain.

Viola stared at her. That green eye. Anne bit her lip. She'd said too much. She knew that look; Viola couldn't help herself. She'd meddle and spoil everything. Ludovic would be livid.

Viola's eye narrowed. "There's something you're not telling me, Anne. Tell me, please. We never used to have secrets."

Anne had been sworn to secrecy. The plan *had* to succeed or she would remain trapped with Ludovic. The Gadgeteers *had* to persuade Queen Victoria to change the laws. Only then could she leave him and return home, for good. And be free.

Anne twisted her teacup on its saucer, and shifted in her seat. But this was Viola. Her sister. Perhaps she would understand. Anne took a deep breath. Surely she could be trusted?

"We're off to London next week," she said.

Viola glanced at Anne's leg. "But...?"

"The *Illusioneer Extraordinaire* has been summoned for a special performance for Queen Victoria, the Prime Minister and selected guests. A double act. Rehearsals begin tomorrow. They don't know. No one does, except Ludovic, his Patron, Marie. And you." Her stomach knotted. "Oh, please don't say anything, Viola."

Viola relaxed. "Is that all? Not declaring a mechanical augmentation without a permit?"

Anne drained her cup. "More tea?" she asked.

"But that's *not* all, is it?" Viola leaned forward. "You can trust me, Anne. I'm your only sister."

Anne cradled the teapot on the tray and stared directly into Viola's eye.

"Promise you won't interfere, Viola," she said.

"I've spent twelve years searching for you. I'm not prepared to lose you again."

"Ludovic is working with the Gadgeteers," she whispered. "They have a plan to gain an audience with the Queen, to convince her to abolish the Mechanical Permits. It all starts with the performance in London. I *have* to be there, Viola. Ludovic *needs* me."

"But do you need him?"

Anne rose from her chair and wandered over to the French window.

Viola rose to her feet. "Anne, if you are discovered entering Britain without a permit, you'll never be allowed to return home. Ludovic is putting your future at risk." She turned to Anne. "I have a friend who will help. He can secure you a permit. Then you don't have to risk exile."

"Why would your friend help me?" asked Anne.

"Because you are my sister. And he is a loyal friend."

"Are you certain?" asked Anne.

Viola nodded. "Then you wouldn't have to stay - out of gratitude, or debt."

"A guaranteed permit?" Anne felt the cold metal of her wedding ring between her fingers. "I'd be free to go home? To stay?"

Viola smiled. "Yes."

Anne closed her eyes and sighed. Her hand trembled. She could be free. She nodded slowly.

"It will be good to see Edinburgh again. It has been too long. Perhaps Father will forgive me. How is Father?"

"He will be overjoyed to see you."

"And mother?"

Viola's smile dropped.

Anne's heart froze. The words fought their way through her lips. "... and mother?"

"Mother died ten years ago."

Anne leaned on the back of the chair by the window. "I didn't know."

She gazed out the window. The grey sky and dismal fog clawed at her broken heart. She glanced down into the street. A dark *fiacre* cab pulled into the *porte-cochère*. Ludovic stepped out of the cab, followed by his financier. Anne gasped and spun on her heel.

"You must go! Ludovic has returned. He mustn't see you here. If he found out I told you about London..."

Viola snatched up her gloves. "Pack your bags. I shall return tomorrow morning. I'll tell my friends I must return to London on urgent family business."

Anne shook her head. "We have rehearsals all day." She peered back out the window. The men had not moved and were deep in conversation. A sliver of sunlight peeked through the thinning fog.

"Come tomorrow night. Nine o'clock. It's Marie's night off and we have reservations for dinner with Ludovic's new partner. I'll say I'm not well."

Anne crossed to the parlour door and listened. All was quiet. She opened it a crack. Marie was nowhere to be seen.

"Tomorrow night, it is." Viola kissed her on the cheek and slipped out the door, into the hall.

Anne eased the door shut, returned to the parlour and looked out the window. There was no sign of either man. Her breath quickened. *Careful, Viola.*

The tea tray rattled behind her.

"*Madame ne reste pas pour le déjeuner?*" she asked.

"*Non.*" Anne twisted her wedding ring. "She had a business proposition. I told her I'd have to discuss it with my husband."

A cacophony of odours wafted down the apartment staircase: onion and stale garlic - the reminders of a neighbour's evening meal - and a whiff of wood smoke from an ill-ventilated fireplace.

Viola wrinkled her nose and tapped on the door. No wonder the

French preferred robust perfumery. How could Anne bear to live here?

The door opened just far enough for her to slip into the apartment. It clicked shut behind her.

"You're late," whispered Anne as she ushered Viola into the parlour.

"I didn't want your concierge to see me," she replied. "I had to wait until she was distracted, reprimanding a young tenant for being overcome by gin." She wrinkled her nose. "All over the entry hall."

Anne frowned. "We haven't got time to amuse ourselves." She picked up a carpet bag and paced the room, examining various trinkets and keepsakes, mumbling and shaking her head. Finally, she took a deep breath and turned to Viola.

"I'm ready," she said.

Viola eyed the bag. She'd always been astounded by how much Polly could pack into hers; how could one fit one's entire life into such a small receptacle?

"Is this all you're taking?" she asked.

Anne scanned the room and nodded. "There are no memories I wish to keep."

She strode to the front entry and opened the door. Viola followed, and started down the main stair.

"Not that way," whispered Anne. She indicated a discreet door at the end of the landing, its outline barely visible in the wall's panel moulding. "There's an entrance to the aquifer tunnels at the bottom of the servants' stairs. They use it to sneak out. Few know it exists."

Viola raised an eyebrow. "I hadn't planned on us swimming back to London," she said.

"We won't get wet." Anne smiled. "There are access walkways and bridges."

"The servants use it to sneak out, you say?" asked Viola.

"Amongst others." Anne hefted her bag and turned toward the entrance. "There are many reasons to avoid the concierge."

Footsteps echoed up the main staircase. Viola grasped her sister's arm. Anne froze. Her gaze darted toward the stairs.

"No, it's too early," she gasped.

Male voices drifted up toward them.

Anne's bicep tensed. "It's Ludovic."

Viola's stomach jumped into her throat. She cursed under her breath. *Botheration.* She glanced at the carpet bag. Ludovic mustn't catch them trying to abscond. She was the oldest; she had to protect her younger sister.

She tugged on Anne's arm, pushed her back into the apartment and closed the door. She needed time to think. She ushered Anne into the parlour and deposited her on the fainting couch near the window.

"Ludovic will be furious." Anne's voice was faint and laboured. "Viola, I—"

"Shh," whispered Viola. She closed her eye and willed her stomach back down. "Let me think." She needed a plan, an excuse for her presence, so Anne would remain blameless. She snatched up the carpet bag and tossed it behind the drapes, behind the fainting couch. She rummaged through her bag, pulled out her tinted spectacles and slipped them over her eye patch. It was too distinctive a feature, and it was the fashion to wear them after dark.

The front door creaked open. Footsteps approached the parlour.

Anne gasped.

Viola placed her hand gently on her sister's shoulder. "All will be well. I'll think of something."

She walked to the middle to the room and concentrated on her breaths.

One.

Two.

Thr—

"Ah, *mon cherie*, you are feeling better? Excellent, we have a guest.

Our new partner has—" Ludovic paused inside the doorway, glanced at Viola and cleared his throat.

His coat fell open as he turned to face Anne. Viola spied the handle of a concealed pistol, similar in appearance to the Professor's pistol. She brushed her hand over her skirt pocket, where it was safely ensconced.

"You have a guest," he said. "You should have told me."

Anne stood slowly. Her fingers trembled.

"Ludovic, I—"

Viola glared at Anne, flexed her fingers and turned to Ludovic. "I must apologise. I arrived without an invitation. I was hoping you would be home at this hour. Your wife has been kind enough to keep me company until your return, though she was obviously indisposed." Deep breath.

"My wife is a strong woman," said Ludovic. "It seems we are to have a full complement of guests this evening." He turned to the doorway.

A short man, in grey suit and gloves, entered the parlour. His dark moustache twitched beneath his grey bowler.

Viola's fingers dug into her left palm, trying not to reveal her horror. A Man in Grey!

"May I present my Patron, Monsieur Gris."

She glanced in Anne's direction. She was pale and visibly shaking. She took a step away from Anne. Had her sister known all along? Was she one of them?

Ludovic eyed Viola. "Amélie, where are your manners?"

Anne licked her lips. "This is Madame..."

"Whitehead." Viola bit her tongue. Why had she used that name?

Anne's eyes widened. Viola glared at her. Was Anne about to panic, or was she going to betray her own sister?

M. Gris smiled. "Yes, the London agent who facilitated the introductions to our new partner."

Ludovic bowed in greeting. "Ah, then fetch us some cognac, *mon cherie,*" he said, "to celebrate."

Anne nodded and stumbled out of the parlour. Viola ventured a steady breath. Anne was safely out of the room; one less thing to worry about.

M. Gris stepped forward and proffered his hand. "I am glad to finally meet you, *Madame.* I am an admirer of your work."

Viola stepped forward, one step closer to salvation, and shook his hand. Her skin crawled at his touch.

M. Gris frowned.

Viola's fingers dug deeper into her left palm. She ignored the urge to run; she had to keep up the pretence, at least until she could reach the front door. Had he met Mrs Whitehead? The Department of Curiosities man, Mr- *Whatever it was today* - had promised to keep the events secret. Had he changed his plans?

Courage, Viola. She forced a smile.

"Is there a problem, Monsieur Gris?" she said in a stern voice.

M. Gris' jaw clenched. "No. I had not expected you in Paris, Madame Whitehead."

He was nervous. He hadn't heard; he had not recognised the fraud. Viola's fingers relaxed. Perhaps she could use that to her advantage, and discover more about their nefarious plans.

"Good. I am glad to hear that," she said, continuing the ruse. "I've been sent to ensure your end of the deal is in order."

The two men looked at each other.

"The English must always be in control, *non*?" There was a faint tremor in Ludovic's voice. They were worried. They were afraid of Mrs Whitehead. Viola smiled.

"Sit down, gentlemen."

They sat on the settee near the fireplace. Viola moved closer to the parlour door. She thought back, recalling Anne's words yesterday.

"Tell me, how are rehearsals?" Viola crossed her arms. "We have barely a week to prepare. I need to ensure all is going to plan. Are you confident everything will be completed before then? I will not endure incompetency."

The Man in Grey nodded. "The Prime Minister is the only one who can get close enough to assassinate the Queen."

Viola stifled a gasp. The Queen! They mean to assassinate the Queen?

Ludovic stiffened. "I will not fail on my part. Then it is up to your man to secure the Prime Minister to the cause."

Viola's heart raced. However, the P.M. would never agree to—

"I am assured she will be dead before Easter, Madame Whitehead," replied M. Gris.

There was a knock on the apartment door. Ludovic excused himself, rose and slipped past Viola to the door. Who could it be? Viola turned to face the window and glanced into the mirror concealed inside the side shields of her tinted spectacles. How much longer could she continue this charade?

Ludovic led the newcomer into the parlour and paused in the doorway, blocking Viola's view. "Do sit down, we were about to have a celebratory drink."

The newcomer sat next to M. Gris.

"I believe you already know Mrs Whitehead?" said Ludovic.

Viola turned to face the newcomer. She stiffened. He scanned her face. Streams of violin music filled her head.

Ludovic's voice droned on: "M. Gris, this is our new partner, Alessandro."

The hypnotist! Pain shot though Viola's eye socket.

Alessandro peered at Viola. His eyes widened and pointed accusingly in her direction.

"I know you. You're that woman doctor. The one with the eye patch."

Viola's hand whipped behind her as she lunged for the parlour door, pushing Ludovic into the hall.

The crystal glasses tinked quietly as Anne carried the tray toward the parlour. She glanced at the front door. So close but, if she ran now, Ludovic would find her. And she wasn't entirely sure she could trust Viola. Maybe the years had changed her?

Viola burst through the door, pushing Ludovic to one side and ramming into Anne. The tray clattered on the polished wood floor. Glasses shattered around her feet. A wave of red wine arced across the hall and sploshed onto the floor, washing pieces of glass under the furniture.

Viola grabbed Anne's wrist and dragged her to the front door.

Anne struggled to free herself. "Let go of me!"

Viola clasped her hand over Anne's mouth as Ludovic pulled himself to his feet, and hauled her out into the hall and into the servants' stairway. She grabbed a lantern perched near the top step.

The stairs were narrow and dark. Wooden steps creaked under their feet as they squeezed their way down. Anne strained against Viola's grip. Her foot slipped and almost sent them tumbling. Anne pushed against the wall, to stop falling, and missed the next step with a thud.

Viola gained her balance, still clutching at Anne's wrist. "Do you want to get caught?" she grumbled.

Anne glared at her sister. "How can I trust you," she hissed. "You work for them."

Viola arms slumped. "Me?" She sucked in a breath. "I'd *never*—"

"But, you said you were—?"

"It was a ruse, to gain their trust." Viola paused mid-stair. "And yours. Anne, tell the truth: do you work for the Men in Grey?"

Anne's breaths quickened. "No." At least not knowingly. "What I told you is true. They promised me they were helping the Gadgeteers."

Viola stepped onto the step above Anne. "Did you know they plan to assassinate Queen Victoria?"

Anne's struggled to catch her breath. "The Queen? No, I..."

"Promise? On your life?" whispered Viola, sounding like a frightened six-year-old.

"Yes. On my life." Anne eyed Viola: she had been particularly good at making up stories when they were children. "But, if you're not working for the Men in Grey," she said, "then how did you know Mrs Whitehead worked for them?"

"We crossed paths at Christmas." Viola leaned closer, gently wrapped her arms around Anne's shoulders and hugged her. "Oh, Anne. I'm so glad I found you."

A door slammed above them. Viola gripped the centre post of the steps. Anne's eyes widened.

"They've found us," gasped Anne.

Viola clasped her hand and hurried her down the steps and into a tunnel carved directly into the rock. The air was cooler and thick with moisture. Water dripped in the distance, echoing each step. They followed the tunnel until they reached a rusted metal hatch with a wheel in its centre.

Viola tugged at the wheel. It didn't budge. Anne grabbed the wheel and pulled with her. It turned with a loud squeak.

Viola glanced back along the tunnel as they pushed on the door. There was no sign of pursuit. The door scraped open.

A faint clunking emanated from the tunnel behind them.

Viola pushed the door closed behind them, scraping her fingers on the bare metal as she floundered for a non-existent handle.

She surveyed the cavern in the flickering lamp light. The fresh water glistened, throwing patches of light across rectangular brick and sandstone columns. Grand arches soared toward the ceiling, like a cathedral.

Their footsteps echoed as they traversed a narrow metal bridge to follow the service walkway running along the edge of the water cistern.

"Where are we?" asked Viola.

"Under *Palais Garnier* I suspect."

Their voices whispered back at them, then faded. Viola winced. Would Ludovic and his Man in Grey have heard the noise?

A large pipe, almost four feet in diameter, followed the raised walkway, dipping under a stepped stone bridge, and continuing into the darkness beyond the lamplight.

"Which way?" asked Viola.

"There," whispered Anne.

Viola peered along the path. Near the edge of the light an outline of a small grotesque carving was just visible, next to a narrow opening cut into the cistern wall. Anne nudged Viola's lantern higher to reveal narrow stone steps inside the tunnel.

The metal hatch scraped in the distance, behind them.

"They're here," whispered Anne.

Viola scanned the water cathedral; they were less than halfway to the tunnel. They'd not make it out before Ludovic and his Man in Grey overtook them. Viola dimmed the lantern. "Can you swim with the mechanical?" she asked.

"No." Anne's gaze skittered back along the walkway and around the cavern. She looked as though she was going to panic.

"Get behind me." Viola stepped in front of Anne. She had to protect her little sister at any cost. Anne must remain Amélie, for now. They mustn't discover her true identity. Anne had to remain in their confidence; Viola had to trust her. Anne *must* live.

Footsteps clanged across the metal bridge, like a gonging death knell.

Viola eyed the crisp water. Where she had to go, Anne could not follow. "No matter what happens, don't let them know who you really are. Promise me you'll go to London. You must stop them killing the

Queen. Tell Sir Archibald Huntington-Smythe you're my sister. He'll help you. I trust you."

Ludovic stepped onto the service path. His Man in Grey and the Hypnotist flanked him, blocking any chance of escape that way.

"So, we have a spy in our midst?" he hissed. "Do you know what we do to spies?" He raised his pistol in Viola's direction.

She clasped Anne's hand and squeezed. "Trust me," she whispered, "older sister knows best."

"Stay back," Viola replied to Ludovic. She slipped her arm up to rest gently around Anne's neck.

"I will not be intimidated, Doctor Stewart," snapped Ludovic.

Viola placed her other arm around Anne's waist and whispered into Anne's ear: "It must look like you attacked me, or we're both dead. And so is our Queen." She felt Anne's muscle tense. "Easy does it. One. Two— "

His pistol's hammer cocked.

Viola spun around, twisting her own arm behind her back as she dragged Anne behind her and presented herself as a supposedly unwilling shield between Anne and their attackers.

The pistol shot cracked through the air, reverberating off the rock wall. Viola's lantern clanged to the ground. Her foot connected with it as she fell into the water with a splash. The lantern skittered across the walkway and plopped into the water behind her, its light extinguished.

Chapter 3: Reveal

Viola's hand reached up into the dark. The ice water chilled her to the bone. Her numb fingers scraped the edge of the walkway and clawed along the stone until they found an edge to grip. She hauled herself out of the water, lungs bursting as she gasped for air. Her teeth chattered. She coughed several gurgling breaths until her lungs cleared.

That had possibly not been her best idea. The bullet catch was risky, even if she *had* practised night and day. But serendipity had presented it as the only way to escape an impossible situation, and save Anne. She spluttered water and made a mental note to thank the Professor for the use of his firearm. And apologise for its loss.

Her fingers slipped on the wet flagstones, tipping her balance. Her foot slipped on the slick bottom of the cistern. The weight of her water-logged skirts weighed her down and dragged her back under the surface.

Viola kicked at her skirts and pushed her feet against the bottom. Throwing both arms over the path edge, she scrambled to regain her balance and stand upright. She rose out of the water and clung to the stone. The water lapped against her bodice.

She puffed the water off her face and coughed again. Water trickled down her neck and pooled under her hands. A coil of wet hair fell across her face and clung to her neck, dripping water into her décolletage.

She wiped the water from her ears and strained to hear the dripping water, recalling the original direction she had first heard it. If she moved to the left, she should encounter the metal bridge near the entrance. Find that, and she could get her bearings to the tunnel Anne had shown her.

A rhythmic clacking filled the cavern. Gas hissed. An engine turned and chugged in the distance. A new water current tugged at her skirts, gently at first but growing stronger with each swell.

Botheration.

There was a soft tapping on her forearm, ebbing with the current. Viola flinched, unable to discern its origin in the pitch black of the unlit cistern. A soft tendril wrapped around her fingers. Her eye patch! She clasped her eye in panic. No eye patch. No tinted spectacles. She felt naked. Her heart pounded as she snatched it and tied it snug around her head.

She side-stepped along the edge of the cistern, hoping she had calculated the correct direction, until her arm slammed into a metal rail. She hugged it and listened for any sound of Anne or the conspirators. The only sound was the constant chugging of the pump engine.

Viola pulled herself onto the walkway at the end of the bridge and lay on her back, catching her breath. She unwrapped the strand of hair, flipped it from her neck and peered into the black void that surrounded her. Her only light source was lying drowned at the bottom of the water. Her shoulders slumped against the cold stone. It had to be done. The Men in Grey could not know she was still alive.

The chill seeped into her shoulder blades and down her arm. She shivered and lifted herself up onto her elbows. She couldn't stay here; she'd catch her death of cold.

She rose slowly to her feet and shuffled along the walkway, feeling her way along the wall to avoid falling back into the water. Her fingers wrapped around the carved *grotesque*. She clung to the sculpture, probed the dark for the tunnel entrance and turned her face to the warm trickle of air emitting from the tunnel.

Viola climbed up the uneven steps, her muscles twinging with each step. A door blocked the top of the stairs. She felt along the door for a latch. Flecks of metal pressed into her fingers and pricked her skin. Rust from the door? She yanked off her gloves and tossed them on the ground in disgust. Another pair of gloves ruined!

She sighed and pulled on the latch. Something in the wall clunked. A grating sound slid from the door into the wall. The door vibrated under her hand, shuddered and clicked open. A chill breeze rushed through the crack. She pushed open the door, shivered and pressed back against the wall to avoid a gust of wind.

Glaring light and the smells of fresh-baked bread, onions and ripe manure assaulted her senses. Viola squinted and waited for her eyesight to adjust to the light. Even this late at night, bright gas lamps lined each shop frontage. Hooves clapped on cobblestones as a carriage trundled past.

Where was she? She felt for her purse. Gone; no money for transport back to the hotel. Her hand flicked to her skirt pocket. The pistol was still there, though likely a little water-logged. She took a deep breath. It caught in her throat. Her lungs convulsed.

She examined her bodice, patted her torso. She picked fine globules of red wax from the emerald silk, examined them and grinned through chattering teeth. After repeated experiments, she had formulated a solution for the bullet catch trick. She chuckled and flicked the wax into the street. *And survived.*

Viola closed her eye, enjoying the familiar sounds of civilisation - horses' hooves, footsteps, the buzz of chatter.

A heavy cloak fell onto her shoulders.

Viola flinched. Her eye snapped open as she reached for the hidden pistol. A pair of brown eyes stared back. Deep furrows formed between them.

"Polly?"

"Miss Viola!" Polly flung her arms around Viola. "I was so worried."

"What are you doing here?" asked Viola.

Polly jumped back and cleared her throat. "Professor Woolington figured out where the sealing wax went. What were you thinking? Do you know people have died performing that trick?"

Viola nodded.

Polly thrust her hands on her hips. "I thought it wise to follow you, in case you decided to do something reckless." She sighed. "Doctor Collins would never forgive me if something happened to you."

Viola stepped over the wooden cross beams and lifted her skirts, careful not to snag the silk on the rough wood. The flickering light of her lantern crept into the uneven corners of the trap room.

The heart of the room had been cleared of most of its theatrical trove to accommodate a moving platform. Several straw mattresses were stacked on the floor of the platform base.

A narrow pulley system, attached to the frame surrounding the platform, led up to an octagonal trap door in the ceiling directly above. Each of its triangular flaps had an attached piston and spring-loaded arm, allowing it to trigger in both directions.

Its wood-handled lever emerged from a bundle of layered wool tied around its workings, possibly in an attempt to dampen the noise of gears and machinery.

A cheap, silver pocket watch hung from a wooden post, a few feet from the platform apparatus. Next to the pole stood an occasional table. A second, smaller trap door had been cut into the ceiling, where the front of the stage would be. A shallow basket had been placed on the table. An empty birdcage sat at its feet.

Viola licked her lips. She picked up the cage. How had Ludovic, the *Illusioneer Extraordinaire*, made it disappear? She examined the cage; each rectangular side had flexible hinges. She raised an eyebrow, and scraped a small fleck of rust off one of the bars. How careless of Ludovic not to maintain his— She grimaced, dropped the cage at her feet and wiped her fingers. Best not to think about it...

She turned her attention to the area on the other side of the platform. Three temporary walls had been constructed, creating a private niche - much like a bird Hide - with its opening facing away from both the platform and the table. Inside, two chairs sat on either side of a small card table.

Floor boards creaked above Viola's head. She checked her pendant watch and shoved it under her bodice. There was no time left for detectiving. Henry and Constable Jones had finally arrived. And they were late.

Viola picked her way around dusty costume trunks and storage crates crammed around the edges of the room, searching for a place of concealment with a good view of both the platform and inside the 'Hide'. She paused and lifted her lantern to get her bearings. Cobwebs clung to her face as she ducked under a low-hanging beam. She shivered, and scraped them off in disgust.

The stage stair door creaked open behind her. Viola crouched behind the nearest trunk and dimmed her lantern.

A rectangle of dim light erupted in the far corner. The sound of footfalls crossed the room. There was a scuffle, a thud, a whispered curse. Viola stifled a laugh. She knew that voice. She peeked from behind her concealment. Constable Jones led the way; Henry followed with his Doctors' bag.

Viola rose to her feet, revealing herself. "Over here!" she yelled as loud as she dare.

Henry and Constable Jones spun to face her. The lantern swung wildly in Jones' hand. Henry stepped into a low-lying truss and cursed again.

Viola winced. "Are you injured?" she asked as they joined her.

Henry cradled his forehead in his hand. "Only my dignity."

"Oh, you lost that long ago," she whispered.

Viola lifted her lantern. Henry's moustache twitched. His dark mop of hair fell over the red mark on his forehead as he side-stepped storage boxes to join Viola behind a wall of crates. Viola gazed into his blue eyes. They were clear and calm; any anger he'd felt on her leaving for Venice seemed to have melted away. They smiled at each other.

Constable Jones placed his lantern on the nearest crate and rubbed his forehead. "Your sister is a brave woman, remaining in the lion's den as it were," he said.

Viola blinked; the spell was broken. "Has Sir Archibald received any more communiques from her?" She bit her thumbnail. No one had been able to contact Anne since Viola's return.

"No," said Henry. "Since her first visit, the Men in Grey have been watching him day and night."

Viola frowned. "Then she won't know I am not dead."

"You've not been able to contact her either?" asked Constable Jones.

Viola shook her head. Her heart choked. How must Anne feel, having to continue the charade, thinking she was alone? Viola's heart dropped into her stomach. It was all her fault! She'd made Anne think her only sister was dead.

She glanced up at the ceiling. Jones' fellow Constables were waiting above, to do their diligent duty. She took a deep breath. Anne's only hope was The Yard's perilous plan would work.

"Why didn't they just arrest them as soon as they arrived in London?" she asked. "I just hope The Inspector's plan works."

"Scotland Yard needs to know if the Prime Minister is implicated in the plot, or just an innocent party," replied Jones. "And there's still no sign of this supposed partner. What did your sister mean by 'double act'?"

Three quick knocks tapped the stage floor above them. Dust trickled down onto their faces and into their hair. Viola coughed and waved away the particles.

"That'll be one of Inspector Abberline's men," said Jones. "They were instructed to signal us when the Illusioneer, M. Fabron, arrived."

Viola extinguished the lanterns, settled down behind the crates next to Henry and Constable Jones and waited for the show to begin.

The entry door creaked open. Footsteps paused just inside the doorway. There was a pop and a gas light flickered into life. A second light appeared in the Hide.

Viola peeked over the top of the crate. A black-suited figure placed a bag on the table, removed his coat and turned to face them.

Viola gasped. It was Alessandro the Magnificent... "The Hypnotist?" she whispered. "What's he doing here?"

"Shh," replied Jones. "He'll hear us."

The Hypnotist unbuttoned his cuffs, rolled up his sleeves and glanced around the trap room. His shoulders relaxed. He pulled a wooden box out of the bag, placed it on the table and clicked the latch. Glass vials clinked as he opened the lid. He pulled out a leather holster, strapped it to his right arm then syringed liquid from three different vials and gently shook the barrel.

He looked worried. Viola raised an eyebrow. What *was* he up to?

The Hypnotist returned the box to the bag and hid it under the table. He took a deep breath. He fumbled with a rubber tube and finally attached it to the barrel of the syringe before slipping it into the harness on his arm. The other end of the tube was attached to an ornate ring on his finger.

He retrieved his coat, slipped it over the harness and adjusted the sleeves.

Viola leaned against the crate; she remembered that ring. She placed her hand on her left shoulder. Drugs? Of course! There were many compounds that increased susceptibility.

"I knew it," she whispered. "He's a fraud."

Jones put his finger to his lips. Henry clasped her hand and pulled her gently back down behind the crate.

Footsteps clunked down the stair.

"Alessandro, you're here. Are you ready?" It was Ludovic's voice.

Viola flinched.

Ludovic entered the trap room and glanced at the Hypnotist. "I do hope you are as impressive as your reputation," he said.

The Hypnotist slipped his right hand in his pocket, nodded and sat down at the card table.

A cloth covered object dangled from Ludovic's hand, rattling quietly as he walked toward the table near the platform. He placed it next to the basket and lifted the cloth. Three white doves cooed inside a birdcage.

Ludovic leaned over the cage and tapped the bars. "How are my lovelies?" He scooped out two of the birds and secured them in the cage next to the table.

Anne appeared at the doorway, paused and crossed the room, in silence, to hang up her cloak on the post near the Hide.

Ludovic turned to face her. "Ah, *mon cherie*, why so sad? Just do as we rehearsed and it will soon be over. Tomorrow, we are paid and no longer need to behold M. Browne's ill-favoured visage." He chuckled, strode up behind her and slipped his arms around her waist, his back facing Viola's direction.

Anne grimaced. Her neck muscles tightened at his touch. Her lips curled. She took his hand and spun gracefully out of his embrace.

Viola clenched her fingers. She wanted to claw out the blaggard's eyes, to drag him off her sister. A gentle hand rested on Viola's forearm. A warm breath brushed her ear, sending goosebumps down her neck. Henry's calm voice whispered in her ear: "Patience, Vi."

Viola took a deep breath and nodded. Blasted Abberline and his plan.

Ludovic kissed Anne's hand. "And it will be like it was, just you and me. And we will be rich."

Anne smiled sweetly at him, her eyes not moving.

There was a knock at the door. "Five minutes, sir."

"Break a leg, *mon cherie*." Ludovic released Anne's hand, snickered and strode back to his birds, picked up both cages and skipped up the steps toward the stage.

Anne glared at his back, flicked her hand and wiped it on her skirt.

Slivers of light streamed through cracks in the stage floor. Footsteps tracked across the stage floor overhead. A shower of dust tumbled and glittered in the shafts of light.

Viola squeezed Henry's hand. "Henry..."

"I know," he said.

"Patience, Doctor Stewart," whispered Jones.

Strains of violin music drifted down through the floorboards. Viola's hand relaxed. Where did she know this tune from? She closed her eye and hummed a few notes.

"Doctor Stewart, are you all right?" asked Jones.

It was too much effort to reply.

"Viola?" Henry shook her gently.

She'd heard the music before. In Venice, again in Paris, and... She poked her fingers in her ears. *The Hypnotist!* Her head cleared. She leaned close to Henry and whispered in his ear: "It's the music. I've heard it before. It's part of the Hypnotist's method."

Henry rummaged in his bag, removed a wad of cotton wool, balled it up into two plugs and pressed them into her ear canals. The music deadened.

Viola nodded and returned to observe the scene. All was quiet.

Anne chatted, unheard, to the Hypnotist as they stood near the platform. She checked the hanging pocket watch. They both stepped away from the table.

A white blur dropped from the ceiling and, in a flurry of feathers, plopped into it. Viola rose slightly and peered into the basket. A partially-collapsed bird cage entombed a crushed and bloodied bird.

Viola's stomach churned. She'd never really considered how that trick was executed. She flopped down on a small storage chest. Now she could never forget.

Henry frowned. "What's wrong?" he mouthed.

Viola shook her head. "You don't want to know." she whispered.

The spring arm snapped back into the fly tower as the flame sputtered and faded. The dove was gone. He glanced into the stage wings; already the stagehand was moving to set up the next trick.

Ludovic grinned and turned to his audience. A wave of applause washed over him. He breathed in the adulation. All was as it should be.

He stepped up to his chalk mark downstage centre stage, gazed beyond the footlights and projected his voice above their heads and into the house.

"I require a volunteer."

A murmur infected the crowd. Ludovic peered in the shadowy outlines of the auditorium.

"You, sir." He pointed in the direction of where the Prime Minister was seated. "Our esteemed guest. Do you like to travel?" Ludovic's pulse raced. He had to secure the Prime Minister as volunteer; Mr Browne would be watching. If his intelligence sources were accurate, contrary to popular consensus, the P.M. was a curious man, intrigued by the unknown - something he had in common with Queen Victoria. Ludovic swallowed. However, the man was introverted. It would take some cajoling.

There was a shuffle in the front row.

"Me, sir?"

"Yes, you sir." Ludovic spoke the words Alessandro had instructed: "Surely you would assist in a demonstration of the magic of science, and not disappoint your fellow Englishmen?"

Lively voices muttered in the front row. A chair scraped.

"Very well." The reply was barely audible.

There was a knock on the ceiling. The star trap door snapped open. A tantalising flash of golden light flickered in the gaping maw, and the trap door snapped closed, returning the trap room to its gloom.

A blurred shadow tumbled onto the pile of mattresses. Puffs of dust exploded into the air.

Viola stifled a cough and peered at the mound. A dishevelled man with a pale bushy beard and uncertain smile sat up, slid off the pile of mattresses and dusted off his suit.

"The Prime Minister!" Jones cursed under his breath.

"Easy, Jones," whispered Henry. "Remember your training."

"I didn't believe he could truly be involved." His shoulders slumped.

Viola's eye widened. "Perhaps he is innocent?"

Jones shook his head. "We shall see. Scotland Yard wants enough evidence to implicate *all* parties. If that includes the Prime Minister...?"

She bit her lip. However *did* they convince the Prime Minister to volunteer? She'd always thought him a sombre man with a reputation for preferring to control a situation.

"Why else would they have employed the Hypnotist? It's obvious they plan to drug him." She rubbed her arm, remembering her past experiences with unwanted hypnotic drugs. "They can be very persuasive." She turned back to observe the proceedings, hoping Jones' suspicions were wrong.

The Hypnotist stepped forward and shook the Prime Minister's hand. The P.M. flinched, almost imperceptibly.

"Oh, I say that was not the most dignified of landings." He rubbed his hand and scanned the room. "It's all rather mundane behind the scenes, isn't it?"

"I am sorry, Prime Minister. As you can see, sir, illusions are not always as glamourous as they appear on stage." replied the Hypnotist. "I'm a doctor, I'm here to make sure you are uninjured."

He ushered the P.M. to the Hide and sat him on one of the chairs. The Hypnotist seated himself opposite and stared into the P.M.'s eyes.

Anne positioned herself on the platform and rested her hand on the lever beside her. She checked the time on the pocket watch, closed her eyes and took slow, calm breaths.

The Hypnotist's voice murmured seductively, rising and falling. Viola remembered that voice; she shook her head. She *needed* to hear what he was saying.

The Hypnotist stared into his victim's unblinking eyes. "... but she is not who she claims to be. That woman is not your Queen, but an impostor."

"Impostor," the P.M. repeated in a drawling voice.

"It is your duty to save the Empire from this evil deceiver. You must eradicate the vermin. You must kill the woman who calls herself Queen. For the good of the Empire!"

Henry's cheeks flushed. His moustache twitched. "That's it!" he hissed. "We have what we need."

He jumped up and strode toward the Hide. Jones grabbed his pistol and followed.

Anne cringed as they advanced past her. Her hand trembled on the lever. Viola's heart thumped. Anne looked terrified.

Jones grabbed the Hypnotist's right wrist and wrenched his coat half way down his arms, being careful to avoid the spiked ring on his finger.

Henry dropped his doctors' bag onto the table, bent down next to the P.M. and examined his eyes. He gently slapped the P.M.'s cheek.

Anne checked the timepiece again. She swallowed. Viola's heart clenched.

"That's enough!" hissed Viola. Anne didn't need to be put through such torment. Viola grabbed the top of the crate, hauled herself up and over the crate and raced to Anne's side.

Anne gasped, reeling backwards as if hit by a Benz motorwagon. She opened her mouth. No words came. She slumped against the platform's support pole and sobbed.

Viola scooped Anne up in her arms and hugged her sister. "You are safe now. You don't have to stay here any more."

Anne let out a weak gasp. "But... But you were dead... I saw you.

Viola felt Anne's muscles twitch under her embrace. Anne pushed Viola away, her eyes now reddened in anger.

"You let me believe you were dead!"

"Quiet," scolded Henry, "They'll hear you."

Jones turned to face Viola and Anne. The Hypnotist growled and floundered in the Constable's grip. A handkerchief twitched in the Hypnotist's mouth.

"Please get off the platform, Doctor Stewart," said Jones. "Mrs Fabron needs to join the performance."

Anne shook her head violently and grabbed Viola's sleeve.

"Please, Miss. We have our orders," said Jones.

Viola stepped in front of her sister. "Our instructions were to find out if the P.M. was willingly involved in the plot, and to secure enough evidence to convict those who were." She glared at Jones. "Well, he's obviously not a willing party, and you have enough proof." She assisted Anne off the platform. "Therefore Anne is *not* going."

Jones frowned and glanced at Henry.

Henry nodded. "We have more than enough evidence of the conspiracy and the name of the Man in Grey in charge." He smiled at Viola. "Tell your colleagues they can arrest M. Fabron."

A boot tapped the stage floor above them.

Viola relaxed and hugged her little sister. "Anne, you're safe. You're finally home."

Ludovic stood by the pulley contraption and pushed the lever. The gold cloth twitched and rose into the air. The footlights converged toward the transportation cage. Ludovic stepped clear of the contraption and prepared to take his well-deserved bow.

The crowd remained silent.

Ludovic snapped his head in the direction of the cage. He scowled; it was empty.

He stamped his foot and muttered under his breath. "Where are you, *mon cherie*?" He clenched his jaw. *How dare you humiliate me!*

How dare she disobey him! He took a slow, measured breath. No one must know this was not part of the performance.

Movement flickered in the corner of his eye. His gaze swept along the side aisles as he turned flamboyantly to face the restless audience. Several men in dark suits - pinpoints of gold at their chests and crowned with custodial helmets - moved toward the orchestra pit.

Ludovic's gaze rested on a specific seat in the front row; Mr Browne glared back. He rose from his seat, slapped his grey bowler on his head and headed for an exit.

Ludovic swallowed; he was abandoned.

He glanced at the empty cage as he completed his turn, swirled his cape and smiled the smile of the damned. He was ruined. But he would not be captured.

He stepped backwards into the cage, slammed the door shut and stood in the hole in its base, positioning his feet on the centre of the star trap. He crossed his arms and reached into a hidden cloak pocket.

"Behold the greatest disappearing trick of the age." He threw a smoke bomb onto the floor as he stomped on the centre of the trap door. The panels collapsed; he plummeted through the stage floor to the roar of cheering and applause.

The ceiling opened above Viola with a loud thump. Thundering applause filled the trap room. Viola reacted instinctively and pushed Anne away from the platform as she reached for the 'borrowed' pistol in her skirt pocket.

Black and red silk billowed and whirled, dragging wisps of smoke through the hole as it descended on her.

"Ludovic!" Anne screamed.

Ludovic tucked into a ball and somersaulted onto the uneven pile of mattresses.

A stabbing pain shot through Viola's eye, ricocheting down her neck and into her chest. Her heart palpitated. He would not hurt her sister again. She snatched the pistol from her pocket and aimed it at his head. She would be sure he didn't survive. Her heart skipped, relishing the delicious irony that his own weapon would be the cause of his demise.

Ludovic spread out his arms to regain his balance. Smoke trickled through the cracks between the flaps of the star trap and clung to the ceiling.

Henry stepped forward toward Viola. Constable Jones grabbed Henry's arm.

"It's not safe, sir," he said.

"Recognise this?" hissed Viola.

Henry wrenched his arm free and lunged toward the platform. "Viola, no!"

Too late! Ludovic twisted and rolled off the mattresses. His mouth curled in a one-sided smile and, with a flourish, reached into his cape and flung the remaining dove at Viola's face. She dodged backwards and flung her arms in front of her face to ward off the clawing bundle of beak, wings and flapping feathers.

The pistol fell from her grasp and skittered across the ground.

Henry grabbed Viola's arm. "Are you hurt?"

Viola shook her head and tried to push him out of the way. "Don't let him escape!" she yelled as she tripped over a wooden truss, fell backwards onto her hands and assessed the situation. Was Anne safe?

Anne snatched up the pistol. "Don't move, Ludovic," she said. Her hair was dishevelled, her skirt torn to reveal her mechanical leg.

Ludovic froze. He glanced at her prosthetic and smirked. "You won't shoot me, *mon cherie*."

Her hand trembled as she pointed the muzzle at Ludovic's chest. "Won't I?" she said calmly.

"I have always looked out for you, protected you, *mon cherie*." He lowered his hand a few inches. "I—"

"I have a name," she said through clenched teeth.

"My dear Amélie..." He lowered his hand another inch.

"Stop!"

Ludovic's arm froze. His smile faded. Anne raised her free hand and cradled her gun hand. The pistol steadied.

"My name is Anne," she hissed.

Viola struggled in Henry's grip.

Ludovic's eyelids narrowed. "You *can't* shoot me," he said calmly.

Viola held her breath. Big mistake. She knew Anne. She was stubborn. If you said she couldn't do something...

"No, Anne!"

Anne exhaled and squeezed the trigger.

Everyone flinched. The pistol clicked harmlessly. Anne stared at the pistol, mouth gaping. Ludovic's arm fell to his side. He laughed.

Viola growled. A red veil descended over her vision; she launched herself at Ludovic, swung her arm and punched him in his face, sending him flying into the crates with a resounding crack.

Viola, Henry and Anne followed Lord Calthorpe into the Drawing Room.

"I've been instructed to show you the recently completed redecorations, while we wait," Lord Calthorpe said as he crossed the room toward the full-length bay window.

The last of the afternoon sun glinted off the ornate scroll work of the octagonal wire bird cage standing next to an overstuffed round sofa in the centre of the room. Three mechanical birds whirred on their perches, flapped their wings and tweeted in unison.

Viola examined the bird cage closely. Each automaton was hand-painted in unique detail. "Such exquisite workmanship," she said. "Come and look, Henry."

"They were a gift from the Queen herself," said Lord Calthorpe. "The red one tweets Rule Britannia every morning."

"How adorable." Anne's mechanical leg whirred as she joined her sister next to the cage. She sucked in her breath.

Lord Calthorpe smiled gently. "No need to worry, Miss Carrington. You are among friends here." He held up his left gloved hand and flexed the fingers. The mechanical joints whirred.

Anne stared at his hand. A smile crept over her lips. "Thank you again for inviting me to your party, Lord Calthorpe."

"It is my wife's doing, my dear. She's in charge of such matters. We're delighted to finally meet Doctor Stewart's sister."

Anne blushed. "May I ask if it's a special occasion, Lord Calthorpe?"

Lord Calthorpe bit his lip. "I had better let my wife explain," he said.

Viola raised her hand and hid her grin behind her gloved fingers. No-one knew the purpose of the select gathering; Lady Calthorpe had been uncharacteristically discreet, and Lord Calthorpe was not forthcoming. Viola suspected it was to officially welcome Anne to London, now she had the necessary permits to allow her permanent residence.

But then again, Lady Calthorpe rarely needed an excuse; she was famous for her soirees. All of Marylebone society held their breath whenever she was seen to venture out to the printers, or tailor, in preparation for an upcoming social gathering; each hoped to receive a gilt-edged invitation.

Lady Calthorpe had been fussing all week and, finally, the invitations had arrived. Viola had been invited, along with Henry and Anne. There had been no reply from Sir Archibald as to whether he, too, had been summoned to the gathering. Viola frowned. Sir Archibald had been incommunicado the entire week. Perhaps he was part of the party conspiracy?

"I do hope Sir Archibald is not unwell," said Viola.

"He's just running fashionably late, as usual," replied Henry.

"Sir Archibald's preclusion for tardiness is superseded only by that of my darling wife," said Lord Calthorpe. "In the meantime, I do as instructed." He smiled and pulled a lever on the wall, next to the window.

The curtains jerked and clicked as they trundled closed over an unseen pulley system under the pelmet. The gasolier hissed and erupted into light.

Viola's eye widened. "It's automatic?" she asked.

Lord Calthorpe nodded. "And there's no need to call Brooks away from his more urgent duties."

Viola bit her tongue. How useful this would be for the indisposed, or in houses where there are few servants.

Viola examined the gasolier. There were ten etched gas bulbs in all. The light shone off the gold outlines of the embossed thistles on the new wallpaper. "I heartily approve of Lady Calthorpe's choice of colour," she said. "She has impeccable taste, as always."

The butler knocked at the door and stepped into the Drawing Room. "Sir Archibald Huntington-Smythe, Your Lordship."

"Send him in, Brooks," said Lord Calthorpe with a wave of his hand.

Brooks bowed and left.

"Good evening, Lord Herbert." Sir Archibald bowed his head in Lord Calthorpe's direction and he continued towards Viola and Anne. "It's grand to see you again, Viola." He took Anne's hand. "And Miss Carrington..." He kissed her gloved fingers gently. "I trust the paperwork was all in order."

Anne bobbed. "Thank you again, Sir Archibald."

Henry stepped forward and shook Sir Archibald's hand. "Where have you been all week, Archie?"

"I was on official Crown business, Henry." he replied.

"Have you seen the newspapers?" Viola asked Sir Archibald. "It's full of theories on the conspiracy to assassinate the Prime Minister but there's no mention of any plot to kill the Queen."

"Hmm...?" Sir Archibald's attention seemed set on the mechanicals in the bird cage.

She lowered her voice: "Perhaps Lord Calthorpe has heard something?" she asked Sir Archibald.

He placed his hand on her arm and shook his head. "I had a visit this morning. We've been instructed not to speak of the *alleged* risk to Her

Majesty's life. I'm afraid this means you as well, Miss Carrington."

"Alleged?" asked Viola. "Who instructed you?"

"Mr Chester. I had to remind him I've already signed the Official Secrets Act."

A shiver ran up Viola's spine. Not him again; he'd promised to leave them in peace.

Henry's jaw muscle flinched. "That man is like a bad smell," he grumbled.

"And I was instructed to remind you both of certain official documents you have signed."

Lord Calthorpe cleared his throat and turned to the doorway. "Good evening, my dear."

Lady Calthorpe's amethyst silk gown rustled as she crossed the room to join them. Her hair was fastidiously puffed, plaited and crowned with a jewelled hair comb. She smiled.

"May I present Miss Anne Carrington," said Lord Calthorpe.

"I'm glad to finally meet you, Miss Carrington." Strings of beads glistened and hugged Lady Calthorpe's shoulders as she took Anne's hand. "At last, everyone is here. Champagne for our guests, Herbert."

Lord Calthorpe pointed to the wood-panelled section on the lower half of the far wall. "This is my favourite part," he whispered.

Viola examined the carved decorations on the corner of the panel. "But there's nothing there," she said.

He led them over to the panel near a side table and grinned. "Doctor Collins, you do the honours." He indicated a carved rosette in the corner of the first panel.

Henry pressed the metal centre of the rosette. Gears ratcheted inside the wall. The top of the panel clicked open at the centre and pivoted out in an arc, creating a semi-circular shelf in its wake. A concentric track, several inches wide, ran along inside the edge of the shelf and continued back into the wall. The track shuddered and moved. Glass clinked as a

bottle of *Perrier-Jouët* and six spotless, cut-crystal champagne glasses paraded out on the track and stopped before them.

Lord Calthorpe poured the drinks and presented Viola and Henry with the first glasses.

"Outstanding," said Henry as he took his glass.

"Only the finest for our dear friends," said Lady Calthorpe as she raised her glass. "To Doctor Viola Stewart and Doctor Henry Collins who, *finally*, have set a date."

"And about time too," Sir Archibald whispered in Henry's ear, loud enough for Viola to hear.

Sir Archibald winked. Henry's moustache twitched. Viola blushed. She sipped the champagne. Bubbles popped in her throat and tickled her nostrils.

"I expect to see you both for afternoon tea, at least once a week." Lady Calthorpe turned to Viola. "And you can tell me all about your new adventures."

THE END

Acknowledgements

Thank you to my beta readers, David, Sharon and Susan, and to my writing group who push me harder. Thanks to Lynne for her advice on causality logic. And lastly, to Terry and Zena, for their generosity and dedication.

About the Author

Karen J Carlisle lives in Adelaide with her family and the ghost of her ancient Devon Rex cat. She loves fantasy fiction, gardening, historical re-creation, and steampunk and can often be found plotting fantastical, piratic or airship adventures.
Karen has always loved chocolate and rarely refuses a cup of tea.
She is not keen on South Australian summers.

www.karenjcarlisle.com
https://www.patreon.com/KarenJCarlisle
https://ko-fi.com/karenjcarlisle

Follow me at:
www.goodreads.com/KarenJCarlisle
https://www.instagram.com/karenjcarlisle/
https://www.tiktok.com/@karenjcarlisle
https://twitter.com/kjcarlisle

Other works by Karen J Carlisle

The Adventures of Viola Stewart series:
Available in paperback:
Doctor Jack & Other Tales: Journal #1
Eye of the Beholder & Other Tales: Journal #2
The Illusioneer & Other Tales: Journal #3
Also available as eBooks

Other books by Karen J Carlisle:
The Aunt Enid Mysteries
Aunt Enid: Protector Extraordinaire
A Fey Tale

The Department of Curiosities
The Department of Curiosities
Coming Soon
Against the Empire

Also available as eBooks:
Short Story Collections
With a Twist of the Nib: For when time is short
Another Twist of the Nib: Shorter Tales with a Darker Twist
Quarantine Reads: Escape to Adventure

Mrs Hudson Investigates
Mrs Hudson Investigates
Coming soon:
The Case of the Forgotten Letter

Bonus Excerpt

from the first book of the
The Department of Curiosities series,
a lighter set of adventures, set in the early 1880s

A steampunk tale of adventure, a heroine,
mad scientists, traitors and secrets.
All for the Good of the Empire.

Chapter one:
Of Rivals, Surprises and Escapes

I should have left you where I found you," Tillie whispered. She shoved her gloved hand into her coat pocket and pulled out the brass-covered sphere, the size of a large marble. She held it out before her; even in the dimness of the unlit hall, the finely-threaded steel and brass pins inserted part-way into the sphere glistened. Its chain slithered over her wrist as she turned it over. The inner content of the brass sphere was just visible; an amber glass orb fitted snugly into its metal shell. It spun to face Tillie. Its thin wedge-like pupil locked onto her, widening to fill two-thirds of the aperture, as if trying to consume every morsel of available light. She avoided its stare.

"Oh, don't look at me like that," she whispered. "I am not going to fall for that one again."

A clatter echoed down the dark corridor. Tillie froze mid-step. Something thudded on the floor. The sphere's pupil snapped down to a narrow slit. She spun in the direction of the noise. The Chinese urn at the other end of the hall had toppled onto the carpet runner. Tillie squinted into the darkness, searching for the culprit. The hall was empty.

A picture formed in her mind: green eyes, dark fur. She shook her head.

"No, I don't think the Professor has a cat." Tillie looped the ocular ball's chain over her head, allowing it to fall onto her bodice. She hitched up her skirts and anchored them in place with a small leather cord that snaked from the underskirt and latched onto a grommet on her belt. If the unwelcome ruckus continued in the hallway they might need to execute a quick escape; they weren't exactly invited to this party.

Downstairs, the noise of the invited guests crescendoed. Piano music wafted up the stairs; party-goers warbled an unrecognisable tune, conveniently masking the unwelcome noises in the hallway. Everything was ordered and civilised - as it should be. Everyone remained in either the Dining Room or the Drawing room - as was to be expected during a dinner party. Everyone, that is, except the other intruder who had announced his presence by knocking over the Chinese urn at the opposite end of the hall.

Tillie edged backwards. Her fingers searched for the niche under the stairway where she could slip out of sight.

At the end of the hallway a lantern flickered, bobbing slowly as it moved closer. Tillie's breaths quickened. She shrank into the niche and held her breath as her rival's shadowy outline crept past the urn and climbed the staircase up towards the private family rooms. Was he searching for the Professor's secret also? How did he know? She needed to find the workshop before him. She crept out of her sanctuary.

Downstairs, the piano music fell silent. She heard the faint creak of a badly oiled door hinge and the click of a latch as a door closed.

Tillie waited. Had the guests heard the noise? She tilted her head to listen. There were no footfalls on the stairs. The music started again. She let out a slow, measured breath, emerged from her hiding place and sneaked up the stairs, following her rival.

***

The staircase continued upwards, past the family's private floor and beyond the closed door on the right that lead to the servants' quarters and the attic. To the left of the stairs, a short corridor extended forward. Four doors lay beyond, concealing all from prying eyes.

Tillie smiled. She was confident Professor Waldran's workshop was behind one of these doors. He'd want to keep his work close, away from the curious eyes or spying servants. This was their Master's domain; they would not dare intrude without permission.

She peeked along the hallway. There was no sign of her rival. She tested the doorknob to the servants' stair. Locked. He must still be on this floor. Her heart skipped. Had he found the workshop first?

She scanned the area around the doors. The first three door alcoves were immaculately clean; the alcove on the far right boasted a thicker layer of dust on the surrounding floor. It wasn't that one; the Professor would forbid the maid entry to his private workshop. There'd be no dusting, no cleaning… Tillie flexed her fingers as she crept towards the next door. That was the one.

Her shoulders relaxed. Her footfalls fell silently on the soft carpet runner as her pace quickened.

The chain shook around Tillie's neck. The amber eye spun in its metal casing, searching in the direction of the door. Its pupil dilated.

<Yes!> The Orb's unspoken statement echoed in Tillie's head.

Tillie clasped the bauble in her hand and turned it to face her.

"What do you mean '*Yes*'?" she whispered.

The Orb stared back blankly in reply.

Tillie scowled. "I hate it when you are so cryptic."

She retrieved a small brass ear trumpet from a pocket under her bustle and placed it against the door. She strained to listen: a faint scuffle. A short scrape, and all was quiet again. Had the stranger absconded with her prize?

Tillie pocketed the listening device, slowly turned the doorknob and eased open the door.

The Orb's pupil snapped shut. <Danger!>

Its Orb's voice invaded her thoughts. She grasped her head in her hand.

"Shh!" It was an automatic response. Tillie clutched the Orb in her free hand and froze, hoping she'd not betrayed her presence. She held her breath and tried to listen beyond the door. Silence. Then a faint scrape, a flutter, and nothing.

Tillie released the Orb; it fell onto her chest.

A breeze chilled her hand on the door jamb. She peered through the thin crack of the partially-open door. A puddle of pale light fluttered in the shadows near the window. The room appeared empty.

Where had he gone?

"Anything?" whispered Tillie. The Orb usually had an insight on things unseen. But now it lay quiet, its only reply a widening of its aperture.

Tillie glanced along the hall toward the stairs. They were in full view of any latecomer.

"We can't wait here all night." Tillie pushed open the door.

Another rush of cold air greeted her. The far window was open. Parted curtains fluttered in the brisk breeze. Light, from a discarded lamp on the desk, danced fitfully. Tillie entered, closed the door behind her and leaned against the door.

A key nudged her in the back. She grinned. How fortuitous. She locked the door and slipped the key into her pocket.

The Orb twitched. Its thoughts formed in Tillie's mind.

"No, I don't think the Professor would leave the window open at this time of year," replied Tillie.

The Orb whispered again.

"No, he wouldn't leave the curtains open for all of London to see his work in progress." Questions, questions. Tillie rolled her eyes. Now the Orb chose incessant chatter. She was grateful that the rest of the world could not hear it. That would only lead to more questions - questions she could not yet answer.

"Quiet!" she whispered through gritted teeth.

Tillie crossed the room, collecting a poker from the fireplace on the way, and navigated her way through a narrow path between stacks of crates near the desk until she reached the window.

She poked at the curtains. Nothing. Her grip on the poker relaxed. She peered out the window. A sea of slate-tiled roofs stretched in every direction.

There was a tink of breaking tile. A grating sound, near one of the chimneys, caught her attention. Something scrambled in the dark. Tillie grasped the sill and leaned out the window. A lone fleeing figure, barely visible against the night sky, fled over the roof edge.

<Gone.>

Tillie turned back to face the Professor's workshop. "Yes, but hopefully not with *our* prize."

***

A large oak writing desk with a full set of writing accoutrements stood before her. Note papers lay scattered across its surface. Black ink dribbled out of an overturned ink bottle, partially obscuring the handwriting. The liquid glistened in the lamplight as it dripped off the table edge. Tillie tapped her finger on the liquid. It was still fresh. She wiped her finger on the desk blotter and surveyed the rest of the workshop.

Bookshelves lined the wall on the left, their contents encased in floor-to-ceiling glass doors. An octagonal display case sat in the far corner, packed with a collection of curiosities. To the right was a long work bench. A large muslin-covered object sat perched on the near end.

Tillie's fingers twitched. What was the Professor working on? She edged past the crates toward the mysterious object; her foot nudged something under the desk chair.

What—? She bent down and searched the floor under the desk. Her fingers wrapped around a small book. Tillie examined the object under the desk lamp; a notebook bound in red leather. Its paper crackled as she opened it. Inside were diagrams of pulleys and levers drawn in faded brown ink; it seemed curiously familiar.

The amber Orb scanned the pages. Images of a hand and quill filled her mind. <Backwards>

Tillie held the book up near the window and studied the reflection, but was still unable to decipher the accompanying text. Perhaps it was in code? She leaned closer to the lamp to see he markings clearer. Her finger nudged its hot glass globe. She flinched. The book fell onto the desk with a thud.

Tillie held her breath. Had she been heard? She cocked her head to listen. Muffled noises below attested the party was still in full swing, but there was no telling when the Professor would grow bored and retire for the evening. There was no time to dally with this distraction now. She picked up the book, tucked it into the hidden pocket under her bustle and flattened her over-skirt neatly back in place.

She returned her attention to the shrouded object sitting on the workbench. Why would the Professor bother to cover up one of his creations, in his own workshop? She moved closer the intriguing object and licked her lips. Her fingers reached out and brushed the cotton. Tillie's fingers recoiled from the cloth.

The Orb jiggled on the end of its chain.

"All right, I'll look!" Tillie reached out and grabbed a patch of heavy muslin and slowly slid it off the object underneath.

Metal glistened in the lamp light. It was man-sized skeleton made of brass and steel. Tillie's heart jumped. An automaton! The workmanship was exquisite. Her eyes widened. Such a treasure. The cage-like body contained a complicated mass of pulleys and levers. In the place of a heart was a box filled with an intricate arrangement of clockworkings.

Delicate wires led down the arms to the metal fingers with each joint a perfectly rounded pulley.

Its skull was the size of a man's. Tillie leaned over the bench and craned her head to examine the automaton more closely. The back of the cranium was open, exposing more clockwork mechanicals; the front was of solid metal with empty sockets that stared back into her eyes. She moved the lamp closer. Several fine wires emerged from the socket walls, each one ended with a small movable bolt ready to screw something in place; something approximating the size of a large marble.

<Home.>

"Home?" Tillie's voice wavered in reply to the bauble around her neck.

There was a faint click as the Orb's iris pupil snapped shut with a click. <Danger!>

Clicking continued intermittently, evolving into a constant ratcheting.

"No need to repeat yourself," she said.

The Orb twisted on her chest.

If it wasn't the Orb, then…? Tillie stepped away from the bench, tilting her head to determine the origin of the noise. It was…

Tillie froze. The noise was coming from the automaton itself. She screamed and jumped backwards, hit her hip on the edge of the solid desk and overbalanced onto the crates behind it.

Long, metallic digits grasped at the air where she had stood just seconds before. The eyeless skull turned in her direction.

Loud footfalls echoed from the stairs. Tillie's heart raced. The music had ceased. The entire household would be upon her in moments.

<Run!>

Footsteps hurried along the corridor. Tillie spun to face the door. Doors rattled. She stepped back toward the window. The automaton's arms flailed in her direction. Closer. It would be upon her before the Professor reached the door.

"Look what you got us into!" she hissed at the Orb. She eyed the metal man as her fingers fumbled at the curtain behind her, and groped for the window sill.

A hand grabbed Tillie's shoulder from behind, her scream was cut short by a gloved hand over her mouth. Her bustle scraped the sill as she was dragged through the window. Glass rattled as its sash slammed shut behind her. The automaton's metal fingertips screeched against the glass, its grinning skull staring blankly at her.

Muffled thumps pounded on the workshop door.

"I think it would be wise to remove ourselves." The stranger released his grip. "It appears you have alerted the household." He retrieved a metal spike from his shoulder satchel and wedged it into the window frame.

The pounding on the door grew louder.

"It will take them longer without the key." Tillie smiled.

The stranger nodded, assisted Tillie to her feet and led her across the roof. Her rival had now become her protector.

****

Tillie's footing was unsteady on the uneven tiles. "I must congratulate you on your nimbleness," she said.

The man stopped near the chimney at the edge of the roof, placed a metal box on the outside edge of the roof and pressed it firmly. A spike rammed into the brick. Two hooks sprang from the box, inserted themselves between the tiles and clamped onto the roof. He bent down, pressed another button. A metal ladder unfurled from the bottom of the box. Chain clinked as the end hit the cobblestones below.

He reached out to Tillie. "After you," he said.

Tillie peered over the edge. The ladder was a foot wide and looked flimsy - barely strong enough to carry the weight of a young chimney sweep. "After you," she said.

~ **X** ~

The man swung off the roof and scuttled down the ladder. Tillie tested the first rung. It seemed solid enough. The ladder rattled.

"Come on," he said.

Tillie followed him down the ladder, her foot searching for each rung. The stranger eyed her as she descended. Her cheeks burned; she pulled her skirts close, ignoring his offer of assistance when she reached the ground.

"Sir, we have only just met and have not been properly introduced," she snipped.

The man tugged on the chains. The ladder retracted upward. The hooks scraped free of the roof as the contraption fell away from the wall. The man nudged Tillie to one side and caught the contraption.

"I suppose I must introduce myself," he said. He unwound the charcoal coloured scarf from his face to reveal a man in his early thirties with a most impressively waxed moustache. "Professor Nicholas Allington of the *Department of Curiosities*, on loan from the Royal Society. I am at your service, Miss Matilda Meriwether." He bowed.

"How did you know—?"

"Your name?" The stranger's green eyes glinted. "The Department has its ways." He scrutinised Tillie's bustle. "I think you have something of mine that I accidentally dropped?"

Tillie's eyes widened. Such familiarity!

"A red leather notebook?" He held out his hand. "Mine, I believe," His flawless waxed moustache raised with his smile.

The book? The one with the diagrams? Tillie's eyes narrowed.

"It belongs to you?" she asked.

"It belongs to the Crown," he replied.

<No!> The Orb wiggled.

"We may be able to come to an arrangement."

"Miss Meriwether, I was told you were worth watching."

***

Read the entire story in

**The Department of Curiosities:
For the Good of the Empire**

Coming:
Book two of
'The Department of Curiosities' series:
Against the Empire